DISCARD

YA   Rowan, Jennifer L.
947.086
Row   Russia.

CLARK PUBLIC LIBRARY
303 WESTFIELD AVENUE
CLARK, NJ 07066
732-388-5999

Afghanistan

China

India

Iran

The Koreas

Mexico

Russia

Saudi Arabia

Syria

United Kingdom

Nations in the News
RUSSIA

by Jennifer L. Rowan

MASON CREST
Philadelphia · Miami

Mason Crest
450 Parkway Drive, Suite D
Broomall, PA 19008
(866) MCP-BOOK (toll free)
www.masoncrest.com

Copyright © 2020 by Mason Crest, an imprint of National Highlights, Inc. All rights reserved. No part of this publication may be reproduced or transmitted in any form or by any means, electronic or mechanical, including photocopying, recording, taping, or any information storage and retrieval system, without permission in writing from the publisher.

Printed in the United States of America.

First printing
9 8 7 6 5 4 3 2 1

Series ISBN: 978-1-4222-4242-1
Hardcover ISBN: 978-1-4222-4249-0
ebook ISBN: 978-1-4222-7577-1

Cataloging-in-Publication Data is available on file
at the Library of Congress.

Developed and Produced by Print Matters Productions, Inc.
(www.printmattersinc.com)

Cover and Interior Design by Tom Carling, Carling Design Inc.

QR CODES AND LINKS TO THIRD-PARTY CONTENT
You may gain access to certain third-party content ("third-party sites") by scanning and using the QR Codes that appear in this publication (the "QR Codes"). We do not operate or control in any respect any information, products, or services on such third-party sites linked to by us via the QR Codes included in this publication, and we assume no responsibility for any materials you may access using the QR Codes. Your use of the QR Codes may be subject to terms, limitations, or restrictions set forth in the applicable terms of use or otherwise established by the owners of the third-party sites. Our linking to such third-party sites via the QR Codes does not imply an endorsement or sponsorship of such third-party sites, or the information, products, or services offered on or through the third-party sites, nor does it imply an endorsement or sponsorship of this publication by the owners of such third-party sites.

Contents

Introduction 6
1 Security Issues 16
2 Government and Politics 34
3 Economy 54
4 Quality of Life 70
5 Society and Culture 86
    Series Glossary of Key Terms 100
    Chronology of Key Events 105
    Further Reading & Internet Resources 107
    Index 108
    Author's Biography 111
    Credits 112

KEY ICONS TO LOOK FOR

Words to Understand: These words with their easy-to-understand definitions will increase the reader's understanding of the text while building vocabulary skills.

Sidebars: This boxed material within the main text allows readers to build knowledge, gain insights, explore possibilities, and broaden their perspectives by weaving together additional information to provide realistic and holistic perspectives.

Educational Videos: Readers can view videos by scanning our QR codes, providing them with additional educational content to supplement the text.

Text-Dependent Questions: These questions send the reader back to the text for more careful attention to the evidence presented there.

Research Projects: Readers are pointed toward areas of further inquiry connected to each chapter. Suggestions are provided for projects that encourage deeper research and analysis.

Series Glossary of Key Terms: This back-of-the-book glossary contains terminology used throughout this series. Words found here increase the reader's ability to read and comprehend higher-level books and articles in this field.

The grand palaces and gardens in Saint Petersburg are an enduring symbol of the enlightened 18th-century tsars, Peter the Great and Catherine the Great.

Russia at a Glance

Total Land Area	6,601,668 square miles
Climate	Humid continental (European Russia west of the Ural Mountains); subarctic (Siberia); tundra (polar north); temperate (southern steppes)
Natural Resources	Oil, natural gas, strategic minerals, rare earth elements, timber
Land Use	Agricultural land: 13.1 percent (7.3 percent arable land, 5.7 percent permanent pasture, 0.1 percent permanent crops); forest: 49.4 percent; other usage: 37.5 percent
Urban Population	74.4 percent of total population
Major Urban Areas	Moscow (12.41 million); Saint Petersburg (5.38 million); Novosibirsk (1.63 million); Yekaterinburg (1.48 million); Nizhniy Novgorod (1.26 million); Samara (1.16 million)
Geography	North Asia bordering the Arctic Ocean from Europe west of the Ural Mountains to the North Pacific Ocean; broad plains with low hills west of the Urals, coniferous forest and tundra across Siberia, uplands and mountains along southern border regions

Introduction

Stretching across Eurasia from the western borders of Ukraine, Norway, Finland, and the Balkans to the North Pacific Ocean, Russia is the world's largest nation by land area. Russia's status as a world superpower has existed since the end of World War II, and today's diplomatic, economic, and political world climates have often pitted Russia against Western nations, including the United States and members of the European Union. The first two decades of the 21st century have seen questions about Russia's role in world affairs, from its actions in former Soviet republics like Georgia to the annexation of Crimea in 2014, involvement in the Syrian civil war, and potential meddling in the 2016 U.S. presidential election.

Russia's experiences throughout history have shaped the country we know today. Historians pinpoint the establishment of the **Kievan Rus** as the beginning of Russia itself. Under the leadership of Rurik, several Slavic tribes united near Novgorod in 862. The Rurik Dynasty would soon move its center of power to Kiev,

Words to Understand

Autocracy: Ruling regime in which the leader has absolute power.

Détente: An easing of hostility or strained relations, particularly between countries.

Feudal system: The political and social system of the European Middle Ages, based on the holding of lands in return for service to a lord or king, and the relationship resulting between the social classes.

Kievan Rus: A loose federation of East Slavic tribes in the late ninth to mid-13th centuries, under the Rurik Dynasty and centered around the Ukrainian city of Kiev.

Marxist: Relating to the political and economic theories of Karl Marx and Friedrich Engels, considered the basis for socialism.

Tsarist: A system of absolute government rule under a tsar, specifically in Russia until 1917.

in modern-day Ukraine, and the political and geographic scope of the Kievan Rus grew until the 1237 invasion by the Mongols. Though reduced to a state of tribute, the center of Russian power again moved, this time to Moscow. This marked the beginning of the rule of the Muscovite princes; Ivan III (the Great) drove the Mongols from Russian lands, further expanded territorial holdings, and established the first iteration of **autocracy** in Russia.

After a period of political upheaval in the early 17th century, control of Russia shifted to the Romanov family, a **tsarist** dynasty that would rule for over 300 years. Under the rule of the Romanovs, autocratic rule tightened and a marked gulf developed between wealthy aristocrats and the peasant population. The **feudal system** of the European Middle Ages deeply took root in a country that remained politically and socially isolated from the rest of Europe for much of its history.

Enlightenment ideals of the 18th century eventually led tsars like Peter the Great and Catherine the Great to institute social and land reforms and to establish early versions of parliaments that, at least nominally, represented the voice of the Russian people. Technologies, fashions, arts, and sciences that flourished in Western Europe found their way to Russia under these rulers, though the tsars who ruled in this period also focused on the expansion of Russia's military might and engaged in multiple invasions and conquests of areas of Eastern Europe.

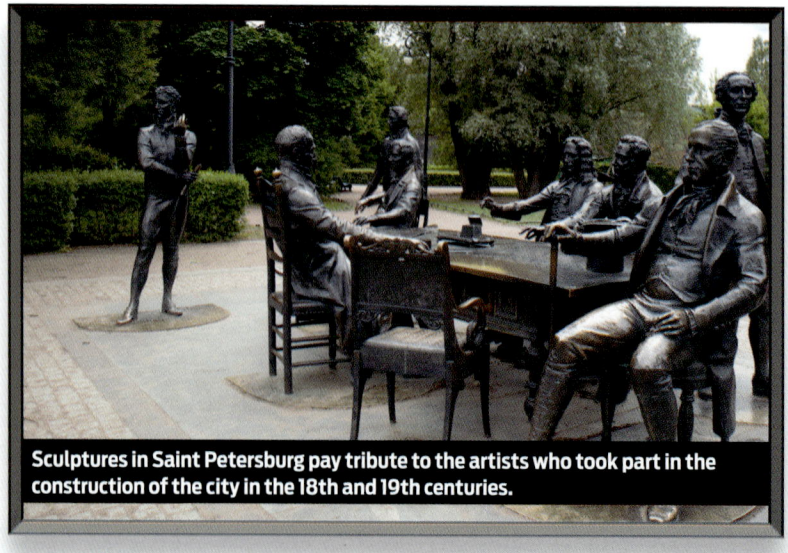

Sculptures in Saint Petersburg pay tribute to the artists who took part in the construction of the city in the 18th and 19th centuries.

Russia's death toll of soldiers and civilians in World War II topped 20 million. This reenactment is one of the ways the memory of that national trauma is kept alive.

Though so-called enlightened despots made outward overtures of reforming Russian government in society, the vast size of the Russian Empire lent itself to centralized rule. But during the second half of the 1800s, the peasant population of Russia began to organize against autocratic rule. The abolition of serfdom in the 1860s and subsequent land reforms did little to improve economic conditions that disproportionately affected common Russians, and **Marxist** ideas began to filter into the country. By the end of Russia's involvement in World War I in 1917, communist ideals had taken hold, leading to the Bolshevik Revolution and the abdication and assassination of Nicholas II. By 1922, the Union of Soviet Socialist Republics (USSR), more commonly known as the Soviet Union, was established under the leadership of first Vladimir Lenin and then Josef Stalin.

Stalin's totalitarian control of the Soviet Union further centralized the socialist government and economy put forth by Lenin in the early 1920s. State-owned farms and industries attempted to grow the Soviet economy, while the government assigned employment to citizens based on needs rather than skills or specialization. Following World War II, tensions between the USSR and the West worsened after Soviet troops remained in Eastern European countries so the Soviet government could maintain control of these bloc nations.

The Cold War era began in 1948, pitting democracy—as embodied by the United States in particular—against the ideals of communism represented by the USSR. For more than 50 years, tensions between the two nations resulted in a nuclear arms race and a space race, involvement in two proxy wars in Korea and Vietnam, and the specter of nuclear war during the Cuban Missile Crisis. The state **détente** between Russian General Secretary Leonid Brezhnev and U.S. President Richard Nixon in the 1970s paved the way for improved diplomatic relations, which ultimately took shape in the 1980s between Mikhail Gorbachev and Ronald Reagan.

Détente in the 1970s.

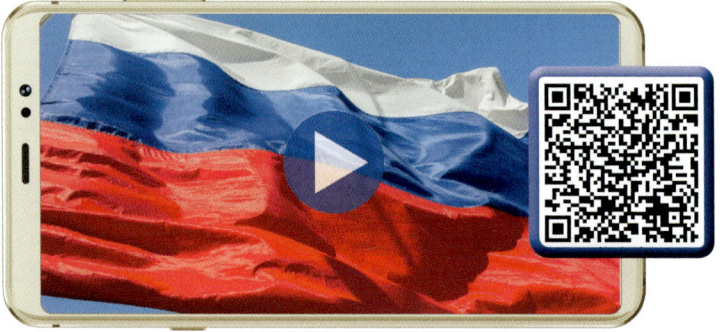

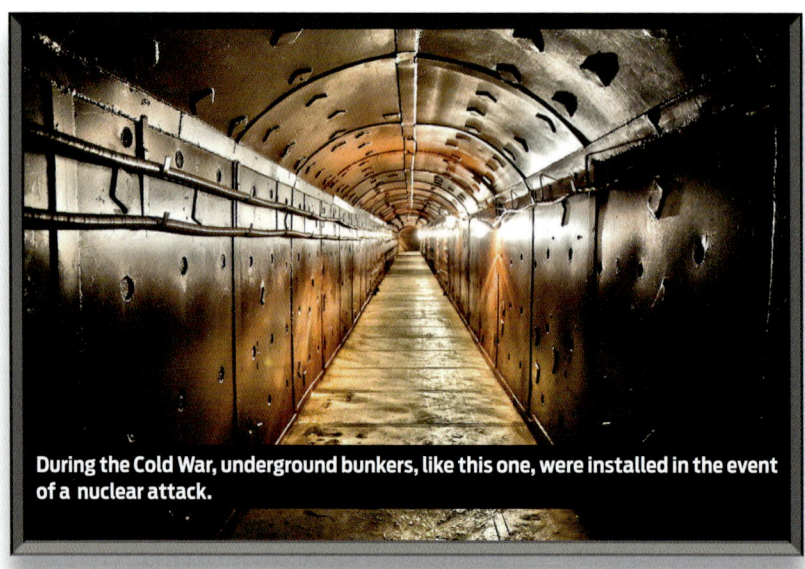

During the Cold War, underground bunkers, like this one, were installed in the event of a nuclear attack.

Nations in the News: **RUSSIA**

Gorbachev shakes hands with President George H. W. Bush in 1990 shortly after the fall of the Berlin Wall.

Gorbachev's attempts to reform a failing Soviet economy in the 1980s would ultimately weaken Russia's hold on the Eastern bloc as one republic and bloc nation after another worked to gain independence. After the fall of the Soviet Union in 1991, the Russian Federation was born, and a concerted effort began to democratize the government and turn the economy toward a more market-based system.

The immediate post-Soviet era saw multiple challenges as the transition to a democratic system unfolded alongside tensions between Russia and some of its territories and former Soviet republics, such as Georgia and Chechnya. By the turn of the 21st century, Russia's economy began to stabilize, even as social issues and political corruption continued to plague the nation. In the era of Vladimir Putin's presidency, the guarantees of democratic processes enshrined in the nation's constitution have come under fire from within. Personal civil liberties, such as due process and free speech, have been increasingly limited by executive order. The government retains control over most of Russia's media outlets, and state-run industries, agricultural lands, and banks are a common feature of the economy. Even election processes have seen change with the removal of local voting for certain regional governmental positions, in the name of preventing fraud and corruption.

Outside of Russia, diplomatic and economic relations have seen their share of stress. Russia is often at odds with Western nations in its role as a United Nations Security Council member and has come up against economic sanctions by the United States and the European Union, most recently in response to Russia's 2014 military involvement in Crimea and the suspected infiltration of the U.S. electoral system in 2016.

Russia continues to work toward a stronger economy and a better image worldwide, despite continued crackdowns on civil liberties, reports of human rights abuses in places like Chechnya, and issues

IN THE NEWS
The Successes of World Cup Russia

Russia won the bid to host the 2018 FIFA World Cup back in 2010, and as the nation prepared for soccer's biggest event worldwide, questions were raised about security for fans and athletes, the possibility of protests or terrorist attacks, and whether Russia would be able to pull off the event with success.

To prepare for the World Cup, Russian metro workers learned basic English phrases to assist foreigners. English signage was added in major thoroughfares and public venues. Service workers received training to impart a sense of welcoming, client-oriented dealings to counter potential misconceptions that visitors may have regarding the Russian people and society. A total of $11 billion was spent to repair and improve infrastructure.

In the end, World Cup Russia was an overall success for all involved parties. No major security issues marred the event, and fans who flocked to Moscow to cheer on their nations' teams noted the hospitality of the Russian people and the atmosphere of camaraderie both in and out of the stadium. Concerns about terrorist activities never came to fruition, and no major protests marred the month-long tournament. The only blight that surfaced appeared to be the stranding of over 200 Nigerian fans in Moscow, reportedly due to either being swindled out of their return tickets or not having obtained return flights in the first place.

Nations in the News:  RUSSIA

Russia successfully hosted the 2010 FIFA World Cup Games after facing international criticism that it could not handle such a high-profile event.

with crime, human trafficking, illicit drugs, and a deteriorating healthcare system. During his 2018 reelection campaign, Putin identified multiple areas of focus for Russia's future growth, including improvements to infrastructure and communications accessibility, better health care, increased wages to combat poverty, and technological advances in industry to improve productivity as well as technology industries themselves.

As the second decade of the 21st century comes to a close, Russia has become a major player in multiple world events, from the ongoing Syrian civil war to the war on ISIS. Its status as a top producer of oil and other important natural resources ties the Russian Federation to world economic trends. While relations with Western nations have faltered in recent years, it bears watching to see if and how Russia's role in the world will lead to more collaboration with the West—or if negotiations on key issues will result in the further breakdown of Russia's relationship with Europe and the United States.

Moscow's Tretyakov Gallery houses one of many fine art collections in Russia.

Text-Dependent Questions

1. How did the ruling methods of the autocratic tsars affect the political ideology of Russian peasants?

2. Explain two ways the Russian government retains authoritarian control over the nation.

3. What has Vladimir Putin identified as areas of focused improvement under his presidency?

Research Project

Choose one of the news articles listed in the "News Headlines" section written from a Western point of view. Find news articles and information explaining the Russian perspective of the event or issue. Write a three- to four-paragraph essay examining how the viewpoints of Russia and the West differ and how they are similar.

Russia in the News in the 21st Century

Trump-Putin Helsinki Summit Won't Bring About Thaw, Pundits Say
Moscow Times, July 16, 2018

U.S. Charges 12 Russian Intelligence Officers for 2016 U.S. Election Meddling
RadioFreeEurope/RadioLiberty, July 13, 2018

Canada Rejects Trump's Call to Let Russia Back into G7
CBC News, June 8, 2018

Russia Banned from Winter Olympics by I.O.C.
New York Times, December 5, 2017

Malaysia Airlines Flight MH17 Downed by Missile Launcher from Russia, Probe Finds
Global News, September 28, 2016

Russia Writes off 90 Percent of North Korea Debt, Eyes Gas Pipeline
Reuters, April 19, 2014

Russia's Crimea Plan Detailed, Secret and Successful
BBC, March 19, 2014

Anti-Putin Protesters March through Moscow
Guardian, February 4, 2012

Russia Ends Anti-Terrorism Operations in Chechnya
Guardian, April 16, 2009

Georgia and Russia Nearing All-Out War
New York Times, August 9, 2008

CHAPTER 1

Security Issues

Russia is not unfamiliar with conflict and issues of national security. From its earliest days, the country has had to protect vast borders and sprawling lands from invasion. Unrest from within tore the Russian Empire apart during the waning days of World War I. The birth of the Soviet Union from the Russian Revolution—the 1917 overthrow of Tsar Nicholas II by the Bolsheviks that resulted in the establishment of a centralized socialist state under Vladimir Lenin—sowed the seeds of international tension and mistrust with the West. The years that followed World War II saw further escalation of tensions as the Soviet Union and the United States plunged into the Cold War. Both countries raced to build up their stockpiles of arms and acquire nuclear weapons. Space exploration became a competition not only for scientific discovery but also to develop technologies for national defense. Regional conflicts turned

Words to Understand

Conscription: Compulsory enlistment into state service, usually the military.

Eastern bloc: Eastern European countries that came under Soviet control following World War II, including East Germany, Poland, Czechoslovakia, Hungary, Bulgaria, Romania, Ukraine, Belarus, Lithuania, Latvia, and Estonia.

Jihad: A struggle or exertion on behalf of Islam, sometimes through armed conflict.

16   Nations in the News:  RUSSIA

The flag of the old Russian Empire looks similar to the modern-day flag, which retains the white, blue, and red stripes.

Russia's Security Issues at a Glance

Military Size	1.03 million active personnel, 2.57 million reserve personnel
Military Service	18–27 years of age for compulsory or voluntary service, 12 months conscription
Military Spending	3.9 million rubles ($61 billion in 2017)
Illicit Drugs	7.3–8.5 million users, estimated
Active Terrorist Groups (home-based)	The Caucasus Emirate (Imarat Kavkaz, IK)
Active Terrorist Groups (international)	Aum Shinrikyo (AUM); Islamic State of Iraq and ash-Sham-Caucasus (ISIS-Caucasus)

into proxy "hot" wars for both nations. All-out nuclear war nearly erupted in 1962 during the Cuban Missile Crisis, an intense 13-day standoff between the two countries over the position of missiles in Cuba, Italy, and Turkey.

The post-Soviet era has not been without its problems. Tensions still exist between Russia and the West. In 2018, the United States and Russia expelled diplomats living in each other's countries following accusations of a Russian-backed poison attack on a former Russian spy living in the United Kingdom. But security issues and conflicts have more often come from within Russia and between the former Soviet republics on its borders.

Conflicts

International and regional conflicts have been part of Russian history for decades. The Soviet era saw uprisings and revolutions in the **Eastern bloc** countries that fell behind the Iron Curtain, the nonphysical but highly guarded border between democratic Western Europe and Soviet-controlled Eastern Europe following World War II. The placement of nuclear missiles in Communist Cuba and the resulting Cuban Missile Crisis nearly sparked a nuclear war with the United States in 1962, and involvement in a war in Afghanistan from 1979 to 1989 resulted in a demoralizing Soviet defeat.

In the post-Soviet era, Russia has sought to strengthen its military and political presence in the world. Memberships in various international bodies, such as the United Nations and World Trade Organization, have resulted in diplomatic disputes, while internal conflicts have evolved as the government seeks to centralize control over various regions and republics in the Russian Federation.

Chechnya and Georgia

Chechnya, a small autonomous republic that is part of the Russian Federation today, is located in the region between the Black and Caspian Seas known as the Northern Caucuses. Multiple conflicts with Chechnya have occurred since the days of the Russian Empire as well as the Soviet era, often marked by ethnic clashes. In modern times, the first Chechen war began in 1994, three years after Chechnya declared independence from the Soviet Union. It lasted for two years and ended with the withdrawal of Russian troops.

Nations in the News:  RUSSIA

A group of Chechen women prays for their troops—fathers and sons—during the first Chechen war.

A second war broke out in 1999, when armed rebels from Chechnya invaded the neighboring Russian territory of Dagestan, resulting in a military campaign against Chechen rebels. Chechnya came under direct control of Moscow by the beginning of 2000. Chechen insurgency has developed in the interim, despite attempts by Russian security forces to eliminate leaders of the insurgency.

Another area where lingering post-Soviet tensions exploded into armed conflict is Georgia. Like its neighbor Chechnya, the republic of Georgia declared independence from the Soviet Union in 1991. But despite this declaration, Russia maintained a military presence in Georgia from 1991 to 2007. The military conflict between the two nations began in August 2008, when Georgian forces attacked Russian-backed separatist forces and peacekeepers in the breakaway region of South Ossetia. After five days of fighting, both Russian and Georgian forces withdrew from both South Ossetia and the region of Abkhazia and recognized them as independent states.

Much like Independence Day in America, Georgia takes part in celebrating its indepdence, too. Every year, parades and parties are held across the country.

Ukraine and Crimea

After pro-Russian Ukrainian President Viktor Yanukovych was deposed during the 2014 Ukrainian Revolution, the Crimean Peninsula became the focus of a brief but critical conflict that continues to be a source of tension between Russia and Ukraine.

The question of Crimean independence was answered by an increased Russian military presence in February 2014. Citing the need to protect pro-Russian Crimeans and stabilize the region during Ukraine's political upheaval, Moscow quickly set wheels in motion that would result in Crimea's parliament passing a referendum for the Russian annexation of the peninsula. Ukraine and the West say this referendum is illegal.

Syria

In September 2015, Russia carried out its first act of intervention in the Syrian civil war by launching air strikes that targeted the Islamic State (ISIS). But the Syrian opposition and many Western nations, including the United States, claimed the air strikes targeted rebels fighting against the Assad regime. Russia has

In 2014, Russia's "Little Green Men" seized Perevalne military base as a part of the annexation of Crimea.

Security Issues

Syrian refugees walking on the Turkey-Syria border after fleeing Kobanî.

IN THE NEWS
The 2016 U.S. Elections

Tensions between Russia and the United States have increased since 2016, as American federal investigators have launched an inquiry into Russian meddling in the 2016 presidential election. Instances of Russian interference have been said to include hacking of the Democratic National Convention's databases, the use of phony social media accounts to exacerbate political divides and spread disinformation, and possible meetings between Russian officials and members of Donald Trump's campaign. The proceedings by Special Counsel Robert Mueller included indictments against 13 Russian nationals in February 2018, though no conclusive evidence points to state-sponsored meddling on the part of the Russian government.

supplied Assad's forces with arms and munitions, particularly fighter jets and defense missiles, and its involvement in Syria has sparked further conflict with the United States over upholding cease-fires and whether chemical weapons have been used on Syrian civilians.

Alliances

Russia participates in multiple world alliances, from the United Nations to the Collective Security Treaty Organization and the Eurasian Economic Union. Parts of the former Soviet Union remain strong allies, especially those nations with many pro-Russian emigrants. Russia also counts China, India, Romania, Argentina, and France among its allies.

While Russia is not part of the North Atlantic Treaty Organization, or NATO, a military alliance of 29 North American and European nations, several agreements exist between the two in regard to cooperation. The Russia-NATO Council was created in 2002 to handle joint security issues and projects, particularly to fight terrorism and drug trafficking. Cooperation between NATO and Russia was suspended in 2014 after the Russian annexation of Crimea; efforts were set in motion in 2017 to reestablish military cooperation.

The Collective Security Treaty Organization, a military alliance between Russia and 10 former Soviet republics, was created in May 1992. Member nations seek to counter cybersecurity threats and information technology crimes; they also conduct joint military exercises in the name of preparedness.

The Eurasian Economic Union (EAEU) was created in 2014 and comprises Russia, Armenia, Belarus, Kazakhstan, and Kyrgyzstan. Its purpose is economic cooperation between member nations, and it provides for the free movement of goods and services, as well as capital resources and labor.

Regional Relations

The Russian Federation encompasses 85 political and territorial entities that are considered to be federal subjects. These range from republics to major cities of federal importance, such as Moscow; *krais* and oblasts, which are geopolitical entities; and autonomous *okrugs* and cities that nominally oversee their own affairs. Federal subjects often exist along ethnic dividing lines. The two most recent additions to the Russian Federation—Crimea and the city of Sevastopol on

A session of the Eurasian Economic Council.

Russian citizens watch the 2018 inauguration of President Vladimir Putin.

the coast of the Black Sea—are not recognized by the international community as being federal subjects.

Relations between the federal government in Moscow and the regions of the Russian Federation are fraught with economic and political troubles. The economy is regionalized, but a good fifth or more of the nation's wealth comes from the area around Moscow. Redistribution of wealth to interior regions, facilitated by the strong central government, keeps the country together on an economic level.

In 2004, Russian President Vladimir Putin stopped the practice of direct elections for regional leaders. Local elections were reinstated in 2012, but they were tightly controlled by the government. Today the president can dismiss regional governors and appoint new candidates in their place. Corruption is a problem for Russia, especially at the regional governmental level, where officials and judges can be bribed by those with wealth. Initiatives like the Federal Anti-Corruption Law are designed to find and remove corrupt officials in law enforcement. State and municipal leaders are required under the law to report suspected corruption and bribery, but laws are not always consistently enforced.

International Relations

Russian foreign policy stems from the legacy of the Soviet Union and the loss of international power that occurred in the years immediately following its collapse. Since the start of the 21st century, economic policies, particularly those focused on strengthening industries such as energy production and technology, have revealed a desire by Russia's leaders to retain Russia's status as a world superpower.

Diplomatic work has occurred to resolve the status of remaining nuclear arsenals that were built in both Russia and the United States during the Cold War, including the New START (Strategic Arms Reduction Treaty), developed in 2010 under the leadership of U.S. President Barack Obama and Russian President Dmitry Medvedev. Russia has also pushed back against Western nations that, from Russia's viewpoint, have sought to control Russian natural resources, reform the Russian government, and alter the fabric of Russian society. Summits between Putin and other world leaders in the past several years, such as the Asia-Pacific Economic Cooperation summit in 2011 and the G8 economic summit in 2012, have sought to determine possible solutions to continued conflict, though the process continues and is in constant flux.

Russia's presence as a permanent member of the United Nations Security Council has allowed it to influence international cooperative measures. The Soviet Union had veto power on the Security Council, a privilege Russia retains today. There has been debate about whether the Security Council's makeup and operation should be reformed and veto power removed. But Russia has been adamant that the current system, and the veto, remain in place.

Human Trafficking

Russia has been identified as a source, area of transit, and destination country for men, women, and children who are trafficked for forced labor and prostitution. Forced labor sometimes involves organized crime, and migrants from within Russia as well as surrounding nations are trafficked for labor in various industries. Women and children are most at risk for sex trafficking.

Russian authorities have been found to be noncompliant with the minimum standards to eliminate human trafficking as defined

In 2013, the G-8 leaders met in Northern Ireland.

Human Trafficking Explained.

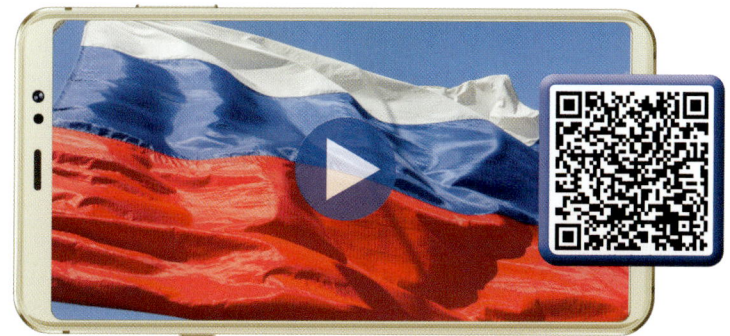

by the U.S. Department of State. Prosecutions are low in comparison to the scope of the issue, and the government has not developed a formal system to identify and help victims.

Illicit Drugs

Illicit drugs are a growing problem for Russia. Cannabis, opium poppy, and methamphetamines are cultivated and sold domestically,

Security Issues 27

while Asian opiates and Latin American cocaine are brought into the country to meet increasing demands.

It is estimated that Russia has the world's largest population of injecting drug users, approximately 1.8 million people. Over a third of that population has been diagnosed with HIV nationwide, with some regions seeing HIV infection rates as high as three-quarters of the local population. Opioid use, particularly heroin, accounts for the majority of drug-related deaths. Drug-related offenses accounted for 63 percent of incarcerations in 2016, and treatment options for drug users are limited.

The increase in drug abuse, especially among young people, has negatively affected Russian society. The majority of drug addicts in 2008 were between the ages of 18 and 30 years old, and many of them had a history of criminal offenses committed to finance their drug use. There is concern for community safety, as those willing to abuse illegal drugs are more likely to engage in prostitution and suffer from homelessness.

An antidrug strategy was launched in 2012 to combat illicit drug use. The "State Counternarcotics Strategy until 2020" aims to reduce supply and demand and endorses legislation to discourage drug trafficking. Four federal agencies exist to investigate instances of drug trafficking, and criminal penalties include up to three years of jail time and confiscation of property and money obtained via drug trafficking. In cases where large amounts of illicit drugs are sold, a life sentence may be handed down.

Military

Branches of the military include ground forces, the navy, air forces, and strategic deterrent forces. The strategic missile force possesses about two thousand nuclear warheads. In addition to acting as a continued national defense, the missile system has also become part of Russia's fight against terrorism. The budget for military and defense expenditures in 2017 was 3.9 million rubles ($61 billion). Major pieces of military equipment began needing replacement or upgrading in the early 2000s, and a good portion of military expenditures has included research and development of new weaponry.

The use and distribution of illicit drugs in Russia is a growing problem. Often, people can be seen on the street using drugs such as cannabis, opium, and methamphetamine.

Members of the Russian army during a training exercise.

In 2018, Russia's military had approximately 3.6 million personnel (1.03 million active, 2.57 million reserves). Russian males must register for the draft at the age of 17 and are eligible for **conscription** between the ages of 18 and 27 for a term of one to two years. Citizens up to age 50 may be obliged to serve in reserve units.

Military personnel have been involved in numerous conflicts beyond the borders of the Russian Federation since the early 2000s, especially in former Soviet republics such as Armenia, Belarus, Georgia, Kyrgyzstan, Moldova, Tajikistan, and Ukraine. Russian forces, ostensibly acting as peacekeepers, remained present in Abkhazia and South Ossetia in 2006, which soured some aspects of relations with Georgia during that time. More recently, ongoing political upheaval and terrorist activity in Chechnya has resulted in various levels of Russian military presence.

Nations in the News:  RUSSIA

Terrorists Attack Schoolchildren in Beslan

On September 1, 2004, 32 armed militants connected to the Chechen separatist insurgency took over control of a school in Beslan, North Ossetia. Over a thousand hostages, most of them students, were held for two days without access to food or water. Explosions rocked the school on the morning of September 3rd, which prompted Russian special forces to enter the building. Over 330 hostages were killed and hundreds of others wounded in the explosions and gunfire that followed.

The targeting of young children shocked and outraged the Russian populace. The Russian government invoked counterterrorism measures. Putin proposed that regional governors no longer be elected through the popular vote but by presidential appointment. In response to the actions of Russian special forces, survivors sued the Russian government over the failure to use intelligence that precipitated the attack, as well as the use of excessive force for the purpose of rescuing the hostages.

Terrorist Groups: Home-Based and Foreign-Based

As in many parts of the modern world, Russia faces the threat of both domestic and foreign-based terrorism. Putin has made the fight against terrorism a priority in his administration.

In past years, one threat of home-based terrorism in Russia came from a militant organization called the Caucasus Emirate. The group organized in 2007 with the aim of establishing an independent emirate, or territory under control of an Islamic ruler, in the Caucasus. The emirate was to be ruled under Sharia law. The Caucasus Emirate swore allegiance to the global **jihad** movement; the leadership encouraged attacks during the 2014 Winter Olympics in Sochi and endorses attacks on civilian targets. After the death of a leader of the Caucasus Emirate in 2013, the group began to splinter. However, the threat of terrorism continues

Russian representatives Sergey Lavrov and Vladimir Putin met with then American secretary of state John Kerry to discuss the situation in Syria in 2015.

as many members of the Caucasus Emirate have defected to the Islamic State of Iraq and Syria (ISIS), which is active within the North Caucasus region.

Foreign-based terrorist organizations include Aum Shinrikyo (AUM) and Islamic State of Iraq and ash-Sham-Caucasus (ISIS-Caucasus). AUM, considered a Japanese "doomsday" cult that includes 30,000 Russians, was classified as a terrorist organization and banned in September 2016.

ISIS-Caucasus may pose a greater threat. ISIS has claimed responsibility for the 2015 crash of Metrojet Flight 9268 and the 2017 metro bombing in Saint Petersburg. More recently, threats of activity from ISIS have targeted Moscow, Putin, and athletes and spectators at the 2018 FIFA World Cup games. These threats and attacks come, in part, in response to Russia's involvement in the Syrian civil war, where ISIS insurgents seek to gain hold of large areas of Syria and Iraq.

Text-Dependent Questions

1. How is terrorism manifested in Russia today?
2. What challenges does Russia face in dealing with drug trafficking and human trafficking?
3. Describe the main roles of the Russian military, including how it is used in neighboring republics.

Research Projects

1. Research the history of the Chechen wars. Write a brief report that outlines the causes of the conflicts between Chechnya and Russia, including how the results of the wars have impacted Russia at home and abroad.
2. Research the causes of the 2014 conflict between Ukraine and Russia over Crimea. Write two editorials, one from the viewpoint of Russia and one from the viewpoint of Ukraine, detailing each nation's position on the conflict. Extension option: Write a third editorial from the viewpoint of Crimea.

Chapter 2: Government and Politics

Russia's current government, established in 1993 after the fall of the Soviet Union, operates as a semipresidential **federation** that follows the principles of **republicanism**. Under this system, executive power is shared by an elected president and an appointed prime minister, while the two-chamber Federal Assembly embodies the legislative branch of government. The judicial branch includes general jurisdiction courts, arbitration courts, and a constitutional court, which is tasked with interpreting laws and resolving conflicts between the executive and legislative branches.

Words to Understand

Federation: A country formed by separate states with a central government that manages national and international affairs while control over local matters is retained by individual states.

Perestroika: A policy of political, social, and economic reforms set forth by Soviet leader Mikhail Gorbachev in the late 1980s and early 1990s.

Republicanism: A political philosophy of representative government in which citizens elect leaders to govern.

State Duma: The lower but more powerful of the two chambers in the Russian Federal Assembly.

Totalitarian: Relating to a centralized system of government that controls all aspects of the state and society.

Members of the Election Commission take part in a Soviet Union legislative election. Before the fall of the Soviet Union in 1993, Russia was a communist country. Josef Stalin's portrait can be seen in the background.

Russia's Government and Legal System at a Glance

Independence	June 12, 1990 (from the Soviet Union)
National Holiday	Russia Day, June 12th
National Symbol(s)	Bear and double-headed eagle
Constitution	Adopted December 12, 1993
Legal System	Civil law system; judicial review of legislative acts
Voting Eligibility	Adults 18 years or older

Throughout its history, Russia has had a strong, centralized government in one form or another. With borders extending from Poland to the Pacific Ocean, the sheer geographic size of the country has, in many ways, necessitated this concentration of governmental power. Under the autocratic monarchs of tsarist Russia, it was considered necessary to consolidate power to maintain security along the borders and the extreme frontiers of the empire. Autocratic rule of this sort was often challenged by revolutionary movements and calls for reform that were brutally repressed. But even the conclusion of the Russian Revolution of 1917 and the overthrow of the tsar resulted in the establishment of a **totalitarian** regime under a one-party system.

Today Russia's government remains mostly centralized, with the majority of state power resting in the hands of the executive branch. Certain areas of the federation retain autonomous control, in whole or in part. The constitution is designed to guarantee citizens the right to the democratic processes of a republic, such as

Viktor Chernomyrdin (*right*) served as the prime minister of Russia from 1992 to 1998. Later in his political career, he served as the presidential adviser to then Russian president Dmitry Medvedev (*left*). Dmitry Medvedev is currently prime minister under President Vladimir Putin.

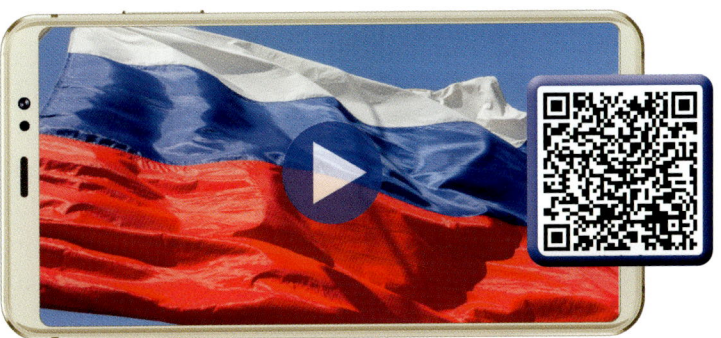

Watch a video overview of Russia's political system and politics.

The Bolsheviks Take Control

In 1917, the people of Russia were angry. The majority of the citizenry lived in poverty; most land was controlled by an aristocracy that ignored the needs of the peasants living on their feudal estates; the tsar and the ruling elite were increasingly despised for the seemingly wasteful lifestyle exhibited at court; and on the eastern front of World War I, the nation was embroiled in a fight against Germany that they were, embarrassingly, losing.

In March 1917, the first stage of the Russian Revolution began. Into the midst of the unrest stepped Vladimir Lenin and the Bolshevik Party. The Bolsheviks' promise of "Peace, Land, and Bread" won the hearts of many Russian peasants. Tsar Nicholas II was deposed, his family imprisoned and later murdered, land was confiscated from the elites, and a peace treaty was brokered with Germany. By October of that same year, the Bolsheviks came to power, with Lenin at the head of the government.

"Peace, Land, and Bread" never truly came to fruition. Civil war erupted between factions of the Communist Party, known as the Red and White Armies. In the end, the Red Army won, and in 1922, Josef Stalin came to power as the supreme leader of the new Soviet Union.

free elections and representation in the Federal Assembly. There is a three-branch system of government, though the checks and balances seen in many Western nations is absent. Power is not shared equally between the executive, legislature, and judiciary, in that the power of the president far exceeds that of the other two branches. Despite a system of plurality, opposition parties have no true influence in the legislature. The judicial system still acts as a "rubber stamp" for the executive, having been slow to move toward independent authority.

The Constitution of the Russian Federation

The Russian constitution was adopted in December of 1993, following the end of the Soviet era. The first section contains nine chapters that establish the three-branch system of government in use today, outline the operation of that government, and enumerate the rights of Russian citizens. The primary purposes of these chapters are as follows:

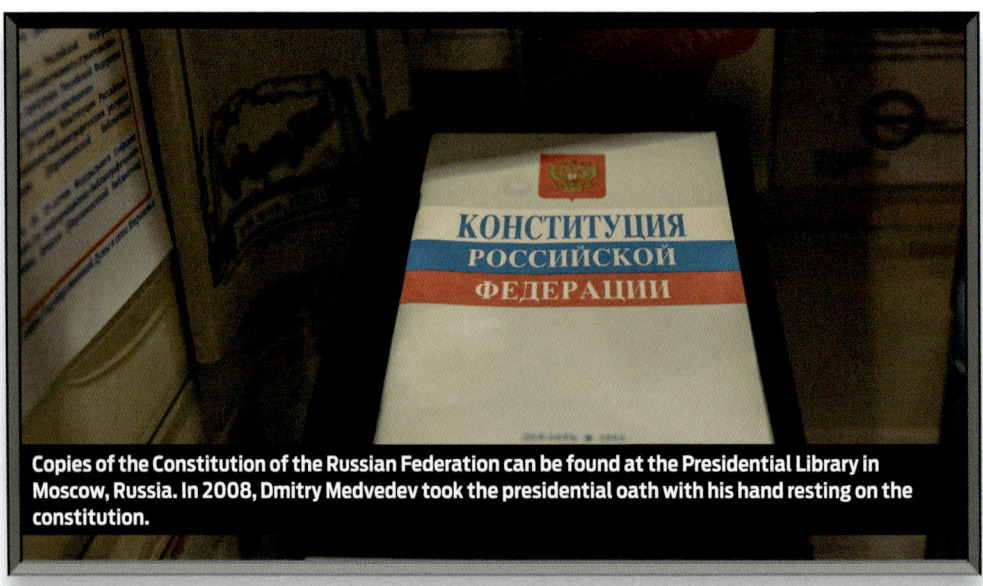

Copies of the Constitution of the Russian Federation can be found at the Presidential Library in Moscow, Russia. In 2008, Dmitry Medvedev took the presidential oath with his hand resting on the constitution.

1. To explain the fundamentals of the system of governance, declaring Russia to be a democratic, federal state bound by the rule of law. Russia is also established as a secular and social state that gives equal rights to all citizens.
2. To establish that the protection of equal human rights, which all citizens are entitled to, is the responsibility of the state.
3. To name and explain the status of all subjects, states, and territories of the Russian Federation, with the main purpose of establishing the jurisdiction of the Russian Federation over its constituents.
4. To declare the president of Russia as the head of state, explain official responsibilities of the office, and provide the president's election criteria and oath of loyalty.
5. To establish and explain the structure of the Federal Assembly of Russia into its two chambers, the Council of the Federation and the **State Duma**. Representation in each chamber is also set forth.
6. To establish the executive power of the government and the authority of the president to appoint the prime minister with the consent of the State Duma.
7. To declare that Russia's judiciary is governed by courts with judges who are independent in their decisions and answer only to the constitution and federal laws.
8. To explain the ability of Russian citizens to choose their local governments, which are responsible for protecting human rights and managing local affairs that include property, budgeting, and taxation.
9. To outline the procedures to be used when making revisions and amendments to the constitution.

The second section of the Russian constitution explains the concluding and transitional provisions, including the term lengths for the Council of the Federation and State Duma. It also states that all members of the government, be they executive, legislative, or judiciary members, will fulfill their duties as outlined in the constitution.

Amendments to the constitution were made in 2008, namely extending term lengths for the president and members of the State Duma. The president's term in office was increased from four years to six and the terms of State Duma members from two to five years.

Creating a Constitution for Russia

In the final years of the Soviet Union's existence, it became clear to Mikhail Gorbachev that to compete economically on a global level, the Soviets would have to make some changes. **Perestroika** became his policy to enact a variety of reforms, many of them divisive among hardline Communist Party members. But that wasn't the extent of Gorbachev's policy changes. He also enacted the policy of *glastnost*, or "openness," which eased the social strictures under which ordinary citizens lived. People were encouraged to speak out, and greater access to information and media was allowed. Finally, Gorbachev began moving toward the democratization of the Soviet Union, paving the way for a new constitution and an elected form of government.

Mikhail Gorbachev was the last leader of the Soviet Union. In 1990, he visited the Russian Embassy in Washington, D.C. Pictured here, Gorbachev waves from his limousine on his way to a summit meeting with George H. W. Bush.

Boris Yeltsin.

When the reins of Russian governmental power shifted from Gorbachev to Boris Yeltsin in 1990, the struggle to create a new constitution grew in earnest. Yeltsin, Russia's first democratically elected president, faced down political coups in 1993 after dissolving the existing parliament—an unconstitutional move in itself. A new parliament was elected that December, and Yeltsin submitted his own draft for the Russian constitution.

The proposed constitution, influenced by democratic principles, sharply differed from the former Soviet system. The drafting process brought ideological divisions to the fore, as various political parties vied for a say in how the new constitution, and by extension the national government, should be formed. Conflict also arose in regard to the separation of powers, especially between the legislative and executive branches, as well as how local governments and the national government would operate under a federal system. Even the constitutionality of Yeltsin's position was called into question because he had declared emergency rule over Russia, ostensibly to prevent Communist leaders from reaffirming control. Ultimately, the convening of a constitutional assembly in May 1993 was required to move the process forward.

Commemorating Russian Independence from the Soviet Union

June 12th marks the date that the Russian Federation declared itself independent from the old Soviet Union in 1990. Russia Day, as it has been officially known since 2002, was originally called "Day of the Passage of the Declaration of the State Sovereignty."

Mikhail Gorbachev's reforms of the late 1980s had begun slowly moving the Soviet Union toward decentralization with the aim of creating a new "Union of Sovereign States." This move was in line with his policy of perestroika, which he hoped would reform society, the economy, and other aspects of the Soviet Union. The reforms and the promise of more personal freedoms for citizens motivated many leaders of individual regions to demand more autonomy over their own affairs. That June, Russia declared its independence from the Soviet Union and became the Russian Federation. A year later, Boris Yeltsin was elected president. A coup attempt occurred just two months later

Nations in the News:

Russian soldiers loyal to Boris Yeltsin prepare to storm the Russian White House in the coup of 1993.

with the aim of saving the Soviet Union; it was put down by Yeltsin and his supporters. From there, other republics began declaring independence, ultimately leaving behind the Russian Federation as it is today.

Russians do not celebrate their independence day the same way people may in countries that have won their sovereignty from a foreign or colonial power. Independence Day in Russia is observed as a state holiday, with businesses and offices closed. Russians spend the long weekend with family and friends. But rather than the boisterous affair that may be seen in countries like the United States, June 12th also serves to remind Russians of the moment when government and society were opened to the rest of the world after almost 70 years of totalitarian control, as well as the turmoil and uncertainty that surrounded it.

Russia's Legal System

The 1993 constitution establishes the Russian Federation as a nation built upon the rule of law, in which all citizens' fundamental rights

Government and Politics

are protected and no one is above the law—a marked change from the totalitarian control of the Soviet system and the autocratic rule of the tsars. Laws and statutes are well defined and codified with the aim of restricting the arbitrary exercise of power on the part of government officials or bodies. Despite the enactment of this legal code, the judiciary remains weak and is riddled with bribery and corruption. Laws are not uniformly enforced, and legal decisions may be influenced by powerful oligarchs, organized crime syndicates, and even high-ranking members of the government.

In Russia, five sources of law create a codified legal system: the constitution; federal constitutional laws; statutes; presidential decrees and agency declarations; and judicial explanations and decisions.

The Constitution and Federal Constitutional Laws

The constitution of the Russian Federation is the highest source of law in the country, having "supreme legal force and direct effect" over all Russian territory. All legal actions must comply with the constitution, whether they are at the federal, state, or local level.

Federal constitutional laws cannot replace those laid out in the constitution but are considered a special type of statute with the power to change federal laws. For a federal constitutional law to be put into effect, a supermajority of two-thirds of the Federal Assembly must vote for its adoption. Federal laws may deal with states of emergency, constitutional amendments, and referendums brought before the houses of the legislature.

Statutes, Presidential Decrees, and Agency Declarations

Statutes are the most common sources of law outside the constitution itself and federal constitutional laws. The length and comprehensiveness of a given statute determines its status as a "federal statute" versus a "code." Flexibility on the part of judges to interpret the language of a statute is necessary for instances in which legal provisions are unclear or there is no precedent due to a lack of court cases.

Presidential decrees and directives operate much like executive orders in the United States or Orders in Council in Canada. Federal agencies must adopt these decrees and directives, but they are considered to be below statutes in the hierarchy of the legal code.

Judicial Explanations and Decisions

Russia's judicial system features multiple levels of courts, and their explanations and decisions become sources of law in various ways. Constitutional Court decisions may determine a law to be invalid, while the Supreme Court can declare administrative regulations to be unconstitutional. Arbitration courts establish legal norms as well as provide explanations of procedural issues, a power shared with the Supreme Court.

The current chairman of the Supreme Court of the Russian Federation is Vyacheslav Lebedev.

Political Parties

A multiparty political system is protected by the Russian constitution to allow voters a wide choice of candidates. There are 76 registered political parties in Russia, though at present only six have any representation in the State Duma. United Russia, closely identified with Vladimir Putin, has become the dominant political party, with members holding prominent positions in the executive branch as well as the State Duma. Several smaller political parties are represented at various regional levels of government.

Prior to 1993, one party, the Communist Party of the Soviet Union (CPSU), had full control of Russia's government. Once the Soviet era ended, however, the CPSU quickly lost power and was eventually disbanded in 1991. Many of its former leaders, however, regained positions of power and authority in the new governmental system over the next two decades. A new version of the Communist Party emerged after the fall of the Soviet Union and retains a consistent second-place minority representation in politics behind United Russia.

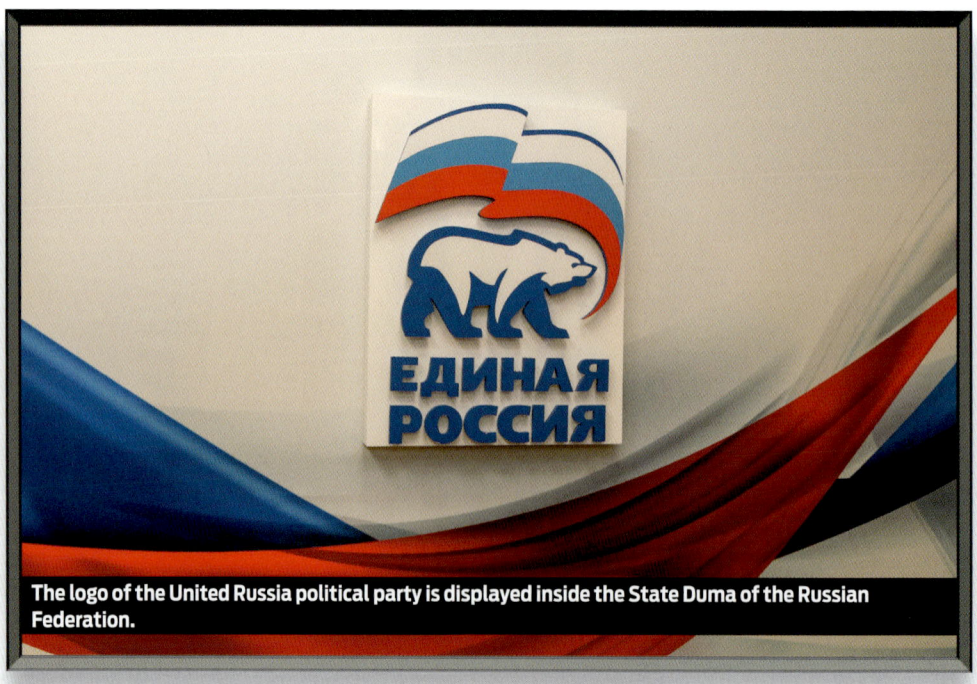

The logo of the United Russia political party is displayed inside the State Duma of the Russian Federation.

The Executive Branch

The dual executive branch of Russia's government consists of the president, who is the head of state, and the prime minister, who is the head of government. Each has specific roles and responsibilities, but the president is more powerful.

The Presidency

The powers of the president are vast. His authority is above all other elected officials. In addition to determining domestic and foreign affairs for the Russian state, the president can also issue decrees and directives that hold the force of law even if they are not reviewed by the legislature. These decrees and directives can be enacted if there is no existing federal law to deal with a given issue. They must not go against the constitution or other laws already in place. The president may also schedule referendums and submit drafts of laws to the State Duma. The president, as the commander in chief of the military, approves defense initiatives and makes appointments to the armed forces high command. He may declare martial law at a national or regional level, as well as states of emergency, though both chambers of the Federal Assembly must be notified in these instances.

Presidential elections were originally set to occur every four years under the 1993 constitution, though this was amended in 2008 to a term of six years. While an individual cannot serve more than two consecutive terms, there are no term limits. Russia has seen this result in the near-continuous leadership of Vladimir Putin. Upon winning his first presidential term in 2000, Putin elevated Dmitry Medvedev into a series of high-ranking government positions. The constitutional rule on consecutive term limits prevented Putin from running for a third term in 2008, but it did not prevent him from endorsing Medvedev as the United Russia candidate. Medvedev proceeded to appoint Putin to be Russia's prime minister. This allowed Putin to gain the presidency again in 2012, since his terms were not consecutive.

Fifty percent of registered voters must participate for an election to be deemed valid, and a candidate must receive more than 50 percent of the overall vote to win. Presidential candidates must be Russian citizens, at least 35 years old, and have lived in Russia for at least 10 years. If the serving president becomes unable to fulfill the duties of the office due to health problems, death, impeachment,

Voters review the list of deputies in the State Duma elections.

IN THE NEWS

Vladimir Putin's Term-Limit Workaround

The lack of term limits allows individuals to serve unlimited terms as president—provided they take a break every two terms. Vladimir Putin first ascended to the top of the political ladder in 1999, when he became prime minister. Boris Yeltsin declared him to be the acting president, paving the way for an election win in 2000 and again in 2004. Adhering to the constitutional rules of the office, Putin stepped down from the presidency at the end of his second term. He would, however, go on to again be appointed prime minister in 2008. This allowed him to run for a third presidential term in 2012, and he won his fourth election in 2018. Putin has stated his intent to step down at the end of his current term in 2024. But current election law would allow him to run again in 2030.

Nations in the News: **RUSSIA**

or resignation, the Council of the Federation must set a date for a new election within three months.

The Role of the Prime Minister and the Government

The prime minister of the Russian Federation is appointed by the president and approved by the State Duma. He acts as the head of government and as such may nominate the deputy and federal ministers that run the government. The system is similar to the cabinet structure common in many Western governments.

The prime minister must administer the business of the state while adhering to the constitution, laws, and presidential decrees. Under his supervision, the ministries and departments that make up the government are responsible for executing monetary policies, foreign policy, state security functions, the protection of property and human rights, and crime prevention.

The Legislative Branch

Legislative power in Russia lies with the Federal Assembly. This parliament has a bicameral, or two-chamber, structure. The Council of the Federation acts as the upper chamber, and the State Duma acts as the lower chamber.

The upper chamber of the Federal Assembly, known as the Council of the Federation, consists of two representatives from every republic, province, and territory of the Russian Federation. Representatives deal with internal issues at a subnational level, confirm justices to the various Russian courts, and also examine and vote on bills that have been passed by the State Duma. These bills can be vetoed, but the vetoes can be overruled if the State Duma insists upon their passage.

The State Duma, despite being the "lower" house in the Federal Assembly, holds the vast majority of legislative power. It is tasked with confirming the president's appointment of the prime minister, appointing and dismissing various chairmen of government agencies and ministries, and reviewing the executive branch's annual report. All bills and proposed laws must be reviewed and approved by the State Duma before they may move on to the Council of the Federation. The State Duma has the power to overrule a veto by the Council.

President Vladimir Putin and Prime Minister Dmitry Medvedev.

A Powerless Legislature

While various legislative bodies were created and dissolved throughout Russian history, the State Duma as it is understood today was first created by Tsar Nicholas II in 1905, in response to that year's revolution. The establishment of the State Duma was supposed to provide a voice for the citizens of Russia. But Nicholas retained extreme authority over the Duma he created, and within a year he dismissed it. The Imperial State Duma was again elected in 1906, 1907, and 1912, before being dismissed again during the 1917 Russian Revolution.

Tsar Nicholas II, the last imperial ruler of Russia, created the State Duma before he was overthrown.

Though the Federal Assembly has multiple powers that ostensibly affect the executive branch, the legislature is subordinate to the president of Russia. The president has the power to dissolve the Federal Assembly.

The Judicial Branch

Judicial reform in Russia had a slow start in the early to mid-1990s. One of the first major reforms was the right of trial by jury. Prior to a 1992 provision allowing trial by jury, judicial decisions were made in "trial by judge" systems.

Under the 1993 constitution, Russia's judicial branch is separated into constitutional, arbitration, and general jurisdiction courts, the last of which are further separated into municipal, regional, and supreme courts of subjects of the Russian Federation.

The courts retain specific duties depending on their type. Constitutional courts evaluate laws and presidential decrees and directives, making interpretations for their constitutionality. Any laws, decrees, or directives found to be unconstitutional may be overturned. The president appoints judges to the constitutional courts, and the Council of the Federation confirms the appointments. General jurisdiction courts deal with civil and criminal disputes, while arbitration courts settle disputes over property or commercial issues.

The Constitutional Court of the Russian Federation.

Text-Dependent Questions

1. What challenges did Gorbachev and Yeltsin face when moving Russia toward the passage of its new constitution?
2. How did Vladimir Putin get around the constitutional rule on consecutive term limits?

Research Project

Research the key elements of the Soviet government and legal system, and compare and contrast them with the current Russian government and legal system. Create a media presentation (video, PowerPoint, etc.) to share the similarities and differences between present-day and Soviet-era Russia. Be sure to include your analysis of how Russia's shift to a democratic form of government has played out in actuality.

Russian citizens receiving ballots to vote.

CHAPTER 3
Economy

Russia's economy is a partial-market system, in that private ownership of industries and property exists alongside a relatively high level of government regulation and subsidization. Radical economic reforms following the collapse of the Soviet Union in the 1990s were ambitious but difficult to implement, especially as multiple financial crises hit Russia in both the late 1990s and 2010s.

Major commodity exports like oil have become the backbone of Russia's economy. These exports, along with measures like tax reforms and incentives for businesses to reinvest their profits

Words to Understand

Collectivism: The practice of the ownership of land and means of production by the people or the state, which resulted in government-owned and -operated industries and farms in the Soviet Union.

Commodities: Raw materials or agricultural products that can be bought and sold.

Gross Domestic Product (GDP): The total value of goods and services a country produces in a given time frame.

Sanctions: Commercial financial penalties imposed on one nation by another, often as a form of punishment or retaliation.

Subsistence: The state of having just enough money or food to stay alive.

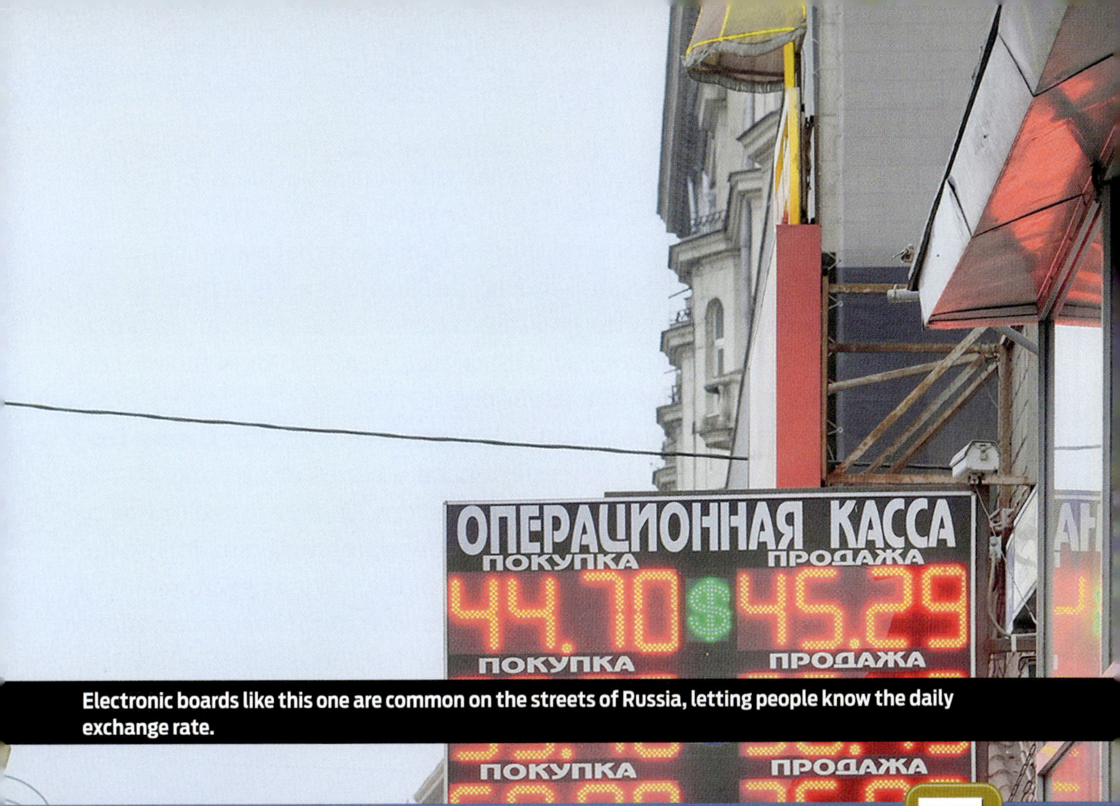

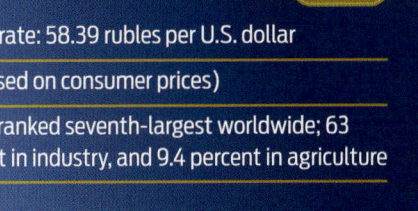

Electronic boards like this one are common on the streets of Russia, letting people know the daily exchange rate.

Russia's Economy at a Glance

Currency	Russian rubles; 2017 exchange rate: 58.39 rubles per U.S. dollar
Inflation Rate	4.2 percent (2017 estimate, based on consumer prices)
Labor Force	76.53 million (2017 estimate); ranked seventh-largest worldwide; 63 percent in services, 27.6 percent in industry, and 9.4 percent in agriculture
Overall Unemployment	5.5 percent (2017 estimate)
Youth Unemployment (ages 15–24)	15.07 percent (2017 estimate)
Imports	Machinery and computers; vehicles; pharmaceuticals; plastics; medical equipment; iron and steel; fruits and nuts; rubber and rubber products
Exports	Mineral fuels; oil; iron and steel; gems and precious metals; wood; grains; fertilizers; aluminum; copper; electrical machinery and equipment
Commodities	Oil; iron and steel; grains; copper; tea and coffee; soybeans; wine and spirits
Agricultural Products	Grain; sugar beets; sunflower seeds; vegetables; cow's milk; beef and veal
Industries	Coal; gas; oil; chemicals; metals; defense industries; shipbuilding; transportation equipment; machinery; textiles; handicrafts; communications equipment; electric power equipment; medical and scientific instruments

domestically, have begun to positively impact economic growth. The legacy of the Soviet Union's various "five-year plans"—governmental plans for economic development that were a hallmark of Josef Stalin's leadership during the Soviet era—is echoed in the way Russian leadership has approached fiscal decision-making. Government regulation, subsidies, and bank bailouts have been necessary to stabilize the economy.

As with other aspects of the Russian economy, the **Gross Domestic Product (GDP)** experienced a series of ups and downs during the first years of the post-Soviet era. After an initial dramatic drop, the GDP recovered by 1997 before plunging again during the economic crisis of 1998. Its recovery in the next six years resulted from greater sales of raw materials and natural resources, more investments, and tax reforms. Another fiscal crisis began in 2014, exacerbated by economic **sanctions** imposed by the United States, European Union, Canada, and other nations in response to Russia's

Russia's annexation of Crimea was an event witnessed around the world. Although no military action was taken to intervene, many took to the streets to voice their opposition, such as these protestors in New York City.

annexation of Crimea. Since then, Russia's economy has seen slow but relatively consistent growth.

In 1998 Russia joined the Group of Eight, or G8, an international body representing the top eight industrialized nations in the world. Its membership was suspended in 2014 due to the controversial invasion and subsequent annexation of Crimea, though membership was not revoked. In 2012 Russia joined the World Trade Organization, an international body that oversees global trade, after 18 years of negotiations.

Currency and Banking System

The currency of Russia is the ruble (RUB), which is made up of 100 kopeks (k). Banknotes used most frequently are the RUB 50, 100, 500, 1,000, and 5,000 denominations, with coins available in denominations of RUB 1, 2, 5, k.10, and k.50. The ruble is regulated by the Central Bank of Russia (CBR) and controlled by the Federal Tax Service and the Federal Customs Service. Estimated exchange rates at the end of 2017 were at a value of 58.39 rubles per U.S. dollar, with an inflation rate of 4.2 percent.

After the tumult of the post-Soviet 1990s, the inflation rate—which reached 2,500 percent in 1992—began to stabilize, and the value of the ruble stabilized with it through the early 2000s. Economic sanctions and a drop in oil prices caused a recession to hit Russia in 2014 and 2015, again causing the devaluation of the ruble and impacting exchange rates with the U.S. dollar and the euro. Since the end of 2017, the value of the ruble and its exchange rate with other currencies has slowly improved.

Currency-control legislation does not allow for the use of any currency other than rubles to buy or sell goods in Russia. Non-Russian residents may use any world currency in transactions with Russian residents, but currency-control legislation must be followed.

The Russian Banking System

The Central Bank of Russia (CBR) ensures the stability of the Russian ruble. The CBR issues money and controls the turnover of currency, monitors exchange rates, and sets monetary policy.

By law, rubles must be used to pay for purchases in Russia.

It also establishes rules and regulations for banking operations and oversees the national payment system, as well as controls government budget accounts and international reserves.

Russian banks are overseen by the CBR and must abide by national legislative requirements. The largest banks in Russia are the state-owned Sberbank, VTB, Gazprombank, Russian Agricultural Bank, Rosselkhozbank, and the Bank of Moscow. These banks offer residents access to personal accounts and mortgages, while companies have access to loans, brokerage, and investments. In addition to national banks, a number of international banks and credit organizations operate in Russia.

In 2017, the CBR executed a bailout of Bank Otkritie Financial Corporation, becoming a 75 percent stakeholder, as well as B&N Bank, another large bank in the Russian system. Rapid expansion, international sanctions, declining oil prices, the devaluation of the ruble, and a high number of bankruptcies have contributed to a shaky banking system. By rescuing the struggling banks, the CBR attempted to prevent a financial disaster and keep banks solvent.

The Russian Labor Force

An estimated 76.53 million people made up Russia's active labor force in 2017. Most workers are employed in services (approximately 63 percent), while approximately 27.6 percent work in industry and 9.4 percent work in agriculture. Unemployment rates are high among youths ages 14 to 24 and among women; overall, the unemployment rate is much lower in urban areas like Moscow than it is in rural republics. Some rural areas can see unemployment rates above 20 percent.

The shrinking number of native Russians in the labor force has come from an aging population and skill sets that do not meet the economic needs of the nation. In 2006 the government determined

A team of workers operates heavy equipment while laying asphalt on a street in Russia. Approximately 27 percent of workers are employed in construction and industry.

The Move from the Soviet System to Partial Free Trade

By the end of the Soviet era, an elite group of bureaucrats controlled all resources and decision-making processes. The centralization of the economy that was so key during the early years of the USSR had begun to fall apart, even as leaders like Mikhail Gorbachev attempted to institute economic reforms during the 1980s.

Russia began its move toward a market economy soon after the fall of the Soviet Union, at a time when fiscal stability was in shambles. Boris Yeltsin, the first democratically elected president of Russia, gave a speech before the Russian Congress of People's Deputies in October 1991, declaring his intention to reform the economy into a market system. Reformers prioritized a balanced budget, liberalizing prices and trade, and the overall deregulation of the economy.

The process was a rocky one that saw struggles with the stability of the ruble, soaring unemployment, the regulation of commodity prices and exports, rampant inflation, and the freedom of private enterprise. Much of the 1990s were marked by this instability, including a severe recession late in the decade. Ultimately, the steadying of the Russian economy into a partial-market system (that is, privatized industry with governmental regulation and control) would not truly begin to occur until Vladimir Putin first took office in 2000. Even now, high levels of government control persist in a number of economic sectors.

that expansion of the immigrant labor force would be necessary to maintain long-term economic growth. As a result, Russia has been willing to accept migrants from areas like Kyrgyzstan, Kazakhstan, and Armenia, as well as refugees who have been turned away from the borders of Western European nations. Russian society has not been supportive of this strategy, though non-Russian ethnic groups have gained control of certain sectors of the economy, such as wholesale crop sales in major cities.

At the start of 2018, minimum wage in Russia stood at RUB 9,489 ($166) per month, with a campaign promise from President Putin to raise the minimum wage in May 2018. With a **subsistence** level of RUB 11,163 ($196), more than 20 million Russians live under the poverty line. Putin's raise brought minimum wage to the subsistence level.

Poverty

Russia has seen great fluctuations in its poverty rate over time. The instability of the immediate post-Soviet era increased the poverty rate, as state-run social support services were unable to meet the needs of those living under the subsistence level. Improved income levels in the early 2000s decreased the poverty rate by almost 19 percent (from 29 percent in 2000 to 10.7 percent in 2012). Poverty levels then slowly increased due to fluctuations in wages, prices, taxes, and other economic factors that were linked to Russia's 2014 recession. In 2016, 19.8 million citizens were living in poverty, the highest number in a decade. Poverty levels then declined slightly in the first half of 2017, due largely to declining inflation and rising wages.

In large cities, like Moscow, homeless men and women can be seen sleeping on park benches.

Economy

Three-fourths of Russia's wealth is controlled by only 10 percent of the population, and its middle class has dwindled in recent years. In addition to an increase in the minimum wage, Putin also vowed to halve the number of Russians living in poverty by the end of his fourth presidential term in 2024.

High inflation levels have historically hindered government anti-poverty measures, though a call to overhaul the state welfare system was made in 2006. Welfare agencies are typically run at the local or regional level and face issues with adequate funding and corruption. The national government has made strides to improve the state welfare system, such as increases for child support payments. Levels of poverty vary from region to region; some areas have poverty rates below 10 percent, while others have seen rates as high as 70 percent.

Agriculture

Due to climatic and soil factors across the country, only 32 percent of Russia's land area is conducive to any type of farming. Collectivism was the norm during the Soviet era, and government-run collective farms were not effectively converted to private ownership. Inappropriate crop choices, intensive farming, and overuse of chemicals has depleted the productivity of Russia's agricultural sector. Subsidization at the federal and subnational levels has attempted to boost the potential of privately owned farmland. Many of the old collective farms are still state run, though they are referred to as cooperatives or labor-management farms.

Grain is the bulwark of Russia's agricultural sector, particularly in the Northern Caucasus and the Volga regions. More than half of the cropland is dedicated to cereals such as wheat—the main grain product—and then barley, rye, and oats. Fodder crops are also key, making up over one-third of the sown area. Other major crops include sunflowers, sugar beets, and flax, which are considered industrial crops and major agricultural exports.

Forestry and Fishing

Both the forestry and fishing industries have remained relatively stable in Russia. With the world's largest forest reserves, the timber, pulp, paper, and woodworking industries hold an important place in Russia's economy. Over 40 percent of the country's land area is

Nations in the News:  RUSSIA

More than half of Russia's cropland is dedicated to grain. Combine harvesters, seen here gathering grain in the fields, allow farmers to gather more crops efficiently than threshing by hand.

covered with forests, though logging had threatened the sustainability of forestry as an industry to the point that legislation was implemented in the late 1990s to prevent deforestation. Wood-related products, especially softwood like pine, are key exports.

Russia's access to both the Atlantic and Pacific Oceans has allowed for the development of a stable fishing industry. Factory ships are able to process large catches even in remote locations, and major ocean-fishing ports can be found on the Baltic Sea as well as the Pacific provinces. The Black and Caspian Seas also provide significant contributions to the fishing industry, though fish populations in these seas have been threatened by industrial and agricultural runoff and pollution. There are also multiple inland fisheries.

Industries

During the Cold War, the Soviet Union focused as much as 90 percent of its manufacturing output on defense industries. The economic reforms of Nikita Khrushchev, Russia's leader from 1953 to 1964, and Gorbachev were meant to shift more resources toward consumer industries. Gorbachev, in particular, realized that such

Industrial fishing is a stable industry in Russia. This fishing boat is operating in the waters off Vladivostok.

When trees are cut down by loggers, they are transported via trucks or railway, as shown here.

Nations in the News: RUSSIA

Nikita Khrushchev led the Soviet Union from 1953 to 1964.

heavy focus on military and defense development had caused the USSR to lag behind the rest of the major world economies in terms of production and modernization.

When the Soviet Union fell apart in 1991, Russia began the process of converting state-owned manufacturers to systems of privatized production. Industrial production initially saw a huge decline in the early 1990s. Eventually, successful industries emerged, and Russia's overall industrial output began to improve. Still, growth rates remained slow, and there have, at times, been declines in certain manufacturing sectors. The defense sector has increased foreign sales to countries like China and India. When coupled with a concentration on high-technology products for civilian use and more domestic military spending, this has resulted in higher rates of growth overall.

Major industries in Russia include metallurgy, including steel production; textiles; chemicals; and a growing number of technology businesses. The machine-building industry is another major manufacturing sector, producing much of what the country needs for industrial, agricultural, and transportation outputs, as well as armaments that are exported to other countries.

Watch a Russian news report on the growing domestic microelectronic industry.

Commodities

Much of Russia's economic growth plan since 2000 has been based on the trade of **commodities**. The export of raw materials, such as iron ore, crude oil, natural gas, coal, and wheat, has become the backbone of economic growth. Crude oil accounts for more than 47 percent of total exports, while refined oil is one of Russia's top commodity imports. This reliance on commodities makes the Russian economy particularly susceptible to recessions and other market-based pressures.

Imports and Exports

Russia's largest trading partners include the European Union (EU), China, Turkey, the United Kingdom, the United States, and Finland. Entry into the World Trade Organization in 2012 opened opportunities for increased trade with the EU, a move that would also help modernize the Russian economy.

Main exports from Russia include both crude and refined petroleum; coal; metals such as aluminum, nickel, and copper; and gems and precious metals. Grains, especially wheat, are key agricultural exports, along with lumber and other wood products. Russia also

A floating drill rig, or jack-up, in St. Petersburg, Russia.

exports fertilizers and other chemical products, electronic components, and energy resources such as nuclear reactors.

Vehicles are a major import to Russia, as are computers, communications equipment, and electrical machinery. Pharmaceuticals and medical apparatuses, along with plastics, make up other major percentages of Russia's imports. Iron and steel imports have increased dramatically, growing almost 60 percent from 2016 to 2017.

Energy

Due to the abundance of resources necessary for energy production, Russia is a major exporter of electric power and the largest energy producer worldwide. Oil, in particular, is a key resource, and one-fifth of the world's oil supply is extracted in Russia. Pipeline systems link oil-production sites to domestic regions, former Soviet republics, and several European countries. These pipeline links and demand for oil have allowed Russia to leverage its influence in neighboring republics that were once part of the Soviet Union, as well as impact world energy prices.

Additionally, over a quarter of the world's natural gas comes from Russia. Coal is another major energy resource, but despite

IN THE NEWS
Have Sanctions Hurt Russia's Economy?

Nations have often used economic sanctions to put pressure on each other to political ends. U.S.-led sanctions in recent years came in response to Russia's annexation of Crimea and its role in the ongoing Syrian civil war. These sanctions include restrictions on access to Western markets and bans on oil-production technology exports.

The sanctions and the boycotts that followed led to economic turmoil in 2015. Banks saw the freezing of overseas assets, and many companies had to suspend operations and lay off workers, some needing help from government subsidies to survive. A coincidental drop in world oil prices made Russia's economic problems worse. But within a year, oil prices and the prices of other major commodities recovered and stabilized.

The Russian government took steps to further steady a troubled economy. The Central Bank of Russia allowed the ruble to become fully convertible, which means it could be traded without limitations. This also meant that since commodities are priced in dollars, companies could still earn enough revenue to reinvest in their businesses. The CBR also instituted inflation control, and the government itself adopted a more disciplined fiscal policy.

Eventually, global commodity prices stabilized, and alongside market-oriented Russian policies, the choice by German companies to lobby Chancellor Angela Merkel to lessen the impact of economic sanctions and invest in Russian businesses ultimately weakened the overall impact of the sanctions.

government subsidization, many privatized but unprofitable mines were shut down in the 2000s.

Russian electricity is produced by power plants that utilize thermal, hydroelectric, and nuclear power. The majority of electricity comes from thermal plants that use oil and gas. Nuclear power production saw rapid expansion during the late Soviet era, but a tragic accident at the Chernobyl Nuclear Power Plant in northern Ukraine in 1986 resulted in a sharp decrease in nuclear power development. Electricity produced in Russia is transmitted to the EU via high-voltage lines.

A car assembly lineman at work in Izhevsk, Russia.

Text-Dependent Questions

1. How does the Central Bank of Russia work to stabilize the banking system?

2. What factors have impacted the pattern of growth and decline in Russia's economy since 1991?

3. How has the defense industry evolved since the fall of the Soviet Union?

Research Project

Choose one major Russian commodity or industry. Research its factors of production, its influence on the overall GDP of Russia, and how it has been impacted by domestic and international economic policies. Write a brief report summarizing your findings.

CHAPTER 4
Quality of Life

Russia's quality of life indicators show difficulties stemming from the transition from Soviet society to a more democratic civil society. While the rate of education among the populace ranks relatively high when compared to other nations, indicators like health care, nutrition, and the ability to exercise political and personal rights fall below global averages.

Basic Human Needs

When the basic human needs of a nation's residents are met, the ability of that nation to develop politically and economically begins to strengthen. Responsibility for meeting these needs falls upon the government, but in the post-Soviet world, Russia has struggled to ensure social welfare. While a system of state-run welfare programs exists, it has proven inadequate and inefficient.

Words to Understand

Paris Climate Agreement: An international treaty sponsored by the United Nations Framework Convention on Climate Change that seeks to limit temperature increases in the 21st century through the reduction of greenhouse gas emissions.

Transparency: The practice of accountability, honesty, and openness in governance or business.

Unpotable: Undrinkable; usually in reference to water supplies rendered unsanitary due to pollution.

Nations in the News:  RUSSIA

Russia's strong educational system has produced a literacy rate of 99.7 percent.

Russia's Quality of Life at a Glance

Life Expectancy at Birth	71 years (65.3 years for males; 77.1 years for females)
Maternal Mortality Rate	25 deaths/100,000 live births
Child Mortality Rate	6.8 deaths/1,000 live births
Mother's Average Age at First Birth	24.6 years
Access to Contraception	68 percent of women aged 15–44
Obesity	23.1 percent of population
Poverty	20 million people (estimated); 13.3 percent of population
Drinking Water	96.9 percent of population (98.9 percent urban areas, 91.2 percent rural areas)
Sanitation	72.2 percent of population (77 percent urban areas, 58.7 percent rural areas)
Electricity Access	100 percent of population
Years of Education	15 years
Mobile Cellular Access	161 subscriptions per 100 inhabitants
Internet Access	76.4 percent of population
Broadcast Media	13 national TV stations; 3,300 regional and local TV stations; satellite TV services; 2 state-run radio stations; 2,400 public and commercial radio stations

Nutrition and Basic Medical Care

During the Soviet era, the availability of food was highly regulated and accessible at affordable prices throughout Russia. Soviet policies emphasized the consumption of livestock products, and this gave rise to a belief that a high intake of protein and fat was necessary to maintain health. Agricultural production declined during economic and political transitions of the early 1990s, resulting in a nutritional shift from high-fat animal products to starches as staples of the Russian diet.

Today, the trend of excess protein and fat consumption continues despite the steep prices people must pay for these commodity products. Linked to this is a lingering belief that high calorie consumption is essential. But the lack of food diversity, namely fresh fruits and vegetables, has led to unhealthy nutritional habits.

Adequate medical care can be difficult to access in Russia. Urban areas, particularly cities of high political importance, see the greatest distribution of facilities and medical personnel. Doctors tend to be poorly trained due to substandard curricula in medical education that was introduced in 2012, and a shortage of nurses, specialists, and supplies and equipment contribute to health-care instability. If individuals are wealthy enough, private health-care can be acquired and is increasingly in demand. Declining health care in the early 2000s, a product of a universal health-care system that is not consistently regulated and funded, resulted in the rise of communicable diseases like cholera, diphtheria, and tuberculosis. Though infant and maternal mortality rates have decreased overall in the past 10 years, they remain high compared to other developed nations.

Recent estimates from the World Health Organization found that nearly 60 percent of Russian adults would be considered overweight, while more than a quarter suffer from obesity. Overconsumption of saturated fats, sugar, and proteins has contributed to several health issues, including cardiovascular diseases, diabetes, and cancer.

Water and Sanitation

Over 10 million Russians lack access to quality drinking water, especially in remote and Arctic regions of the country where environmental and climactic factors make access difficult. The water-supply system

The World Health Organization estimates that nearly 60 percent of Russians are overweight and a quarter of the population is considered obese.

is in need of repair and updating; experts estimate that nearly 30 percent of Russia's water pipes need to be replaced. Agricultural and industrial waste, combined with sewage and other forms of pollution, have raised the percentage of **unpotable** water to 57 percent. The Clean Water project, launched in 2006, aims to boost the clean water supply through the application of more modern technologies. Implementation has encountered opposition, as Russian academics view the project as a business solution that came about in response to the privatization of water resources.

Sanitation facilities have improved over the past several years thanks to investments by foreign companies in building water treatment facilities, reducing contamination of the water supply and the prevention of diseases caused by contact with human and animal waste products. Still, less than 30 percent of wastewater is properly treated before being released into lakes, rivers, and seas. Sixty percent of the Russian population still drinks water from contaminated wells, and though wealthy residents are able to purchase bottled water, others are not so fortunate.

Russia's water-supply system is in need of repair and updating with more than 10 million people lacking access to quality drinking water.

Shelter

An increased demand for quality housing in Russia, particularly in more densely populated areas such as Moscow and Saint Petersburg, has prompted a boom in the construction of homes and apartment buildings in the past several years. Eighty-one million square meters of housing were built in 2014, the largest rate of homebuilding since the end of the Soviet construction boom in 1987. Much of what is being built today includes apartment buildings in areas like Moscow.

One hundred percent of the Russian population has access to the electric grid. However, as demand for electricity increases, the centralized system developed during the Soviet era often proves inefficient. Increases in commerce, production, and general consumption require creative maneuvering by plant operators to prevent blackouts. There is a growing interest in moving away from centralized power plants that run on natural gas to renewable sources of energy, especially as solar and wind technologies improve. Since revenues from oil, natural gas, and coal make up such a large part of Russia's economy, however, a large-scale transition to renewables may prove difficult.

Thousands of families live in dilapidated buildings like this one. However, new housing is being developed in areas like Moscow.

Personal Safety

The crime rate in Russia has remained relatively stable, according to government reports. Violent crime may often be concentrated in high urban areas but has seen decreases—homicides dropped almost 7 percent and violent assaults dropped 9 percent in 2016. Violent crimes typically involve bladed weapons and gang activity and target people carrying large amounts of cash or other valuable property.

Acts of political terror have occurred throughout Russia for decades. Recent attacks have taken place in larger cities like Saint Petersburg, where an explosive device was deployed on the metro system in April 2017. Security risks tend to rise during major national events, such as the 2014 Winter Olympics in Sochi and the 2018 FIFA World Cup. While more recent terror attacks have been claimed by groups like ISIS and al-Qaeda, some instances have occurred in response to Russian policies and activities in disputed territories like Crimea and Chechnya.

The Global Peace Index, which has analyzed and ranked the safety of nations since 2008, places Russia 157th in safety out of 163 countries ranked.

People lay flowers and candles at a memorial at a Saint Petersburg subway station after a terrorist attack in 2017.

IN THE NEWS

Suicide Bomb Attack in Saint Petersburg

The April 3, 2017, bombing on the Saint Petersburg metro system was decried as a terrorist attack by President Putin. An improvised explosive device made from TNT blew up as the metro train traveled between two stations on the underground line. A second device was later found at another metro station but was safely defused.

Officials said that a 22-year-old suicide bomber from Kyrgyzstan, Akbarzhon Jalilov, was responsible for the blast and for the planting of the unexploded device. Jalilov's brother and eight other suspects were arrested for establishing links with and recruiting for Islamist militant groups.

Personal Well-Being

The quality of life for citizens of Russia has improved during the second decade of the 21st century. Russia ranks above average in education and work-life balance but still struggles with major indicators of well-being, such as income, jobs, personal security, housing, and health.

Education

Russian society is considered to be an educated one. The literacy rate of individuals age 15 and over stood at 99.7 percent in 2017. Most Russians expect to complete 15 years of education, from primary school to pre-university-level studies. A Russian education focuses on the intellectual, emotional, moral, and physical development of the student and focuses on abilities that will help the student become part of civil society and make appropriate choices for professional education.

The Russian education system is organized and coordinated by the government, which ensures that everyone has access to a free general education. Preschool is available for children under the age of six but is not compulsory. Primary education lasts for four years, followed by five years of general education and then two to three years of secondary education. Upon the completion of primary and general education, students take final examinations

Students give a presentation in a primary school classroom.

that will determine their placement in either secondary general education, a vocational school, or nonuniversity higher education. Ninety-five percent of adults aged 25 to 64 have completed their upper secondary education.

Information Access

The Russian constitution guarantees citizens the right to access information about national and local government activities. A law providing further access to information was introduced in 2007 in response to a push for greater **transparency**. This law was signed in 2009 with an effective date of January 10, 2010. In the meantime, then president Medvedev created a commission in early 2009 that was tasked with reviewing textbooks, documentaries, and scholarly publications for falsification or misrepresentation of recent Russian history.

More than three-quarters of Russians in urban areas report having access to the Internet in their homes, while the figure stands closer to 56 percent in smaller communities. In 2012, the government established a goal of 80 percent home Internet access by 2018, and the state-owned broadband firm Rostelecom was tasked with bringing stable Internet connections into Russian homes. Urban Russians are twice as likely as their rural counterparts to have access to high-speed connections. Rural populations are more likely to have dial-up access. Internet usage and a social media presence are more common among younger Russians aged 15 to 24. Mobile phones are prolific, with 9 out of 10 Russians using mobile phones for personal or business reasons.

Though the Russian constitution protects the right to free speech and a free press, in practice most media outlets are either owned or regulated by the government. Independent television stations have seen their broadcast access reduced or revoked, while news publications have experienced reductions in their ability to report. Internet users also run the risk of fines or imprisonment if posted content appears to threaten national security.

Health and Wellness

Life expectancy in Russia stands at 71 years of age, lower than the world average of 80 years. A deteriorating health-care system

Nations in the News:

combined with high levels of alcohol and tobacco use, depression, and poor nutrition have contributed to these lower life expectancies. The top causes of premature death include heart disease and other cardiovascular issues; cancer; HIV/AIDS; influenza and pneumonia; alcohol, tobacco, and drug use; and traffic accidents.

Russia's suicide rate ranks 16th worldwide. The country experienced 28,814 deaths by suicide in 2017, accounting for 1.53 percent of premature deaths that year.

Watch a report on living with HIV in Russia.

Environment

Environmental protections were enacted after the Soviet era ended, but despite a movement toward cleaner air and water, Russia still suffers from air pollution. Air quality is an issue primarily in major industrial cities. Vehicular pollution is a problem in urban centers such as Moscow. In 2016, emissions totaled 31.6 million metric tons, an increase of just over 1 percent from the previous year.

Greenhouse gas emissions dropped significantly after the collapse of the Soviet Union, but worldwide concerns about the impact of emissions on climate change have prompted policy changes. President Putin issued an executive order in 2016 to begin the process of reducing greenhouse gas emissions. However, commitments to reducing emissions have, so far, not shown sufficient change to meet the parameters set by the **Paris Climate Agreement**.

Quality of Life

Air pollution has many sources, including the chimneys of heating and power plants.

Opportunity

Following the repressive regimes of the Soviet Union and its predecessor, the tsarist autocracy, Russia's goal of a civil, democratic society incorporated ideas of personal freedoms and opportunities. As with other areas of Russian life and society, some of these opportunities have proven difficult to achieve.

Personal and Political Rights

The ability of Russian citizens to exercise personal freedoms and political rights is part of the Russian constitution, but in practice Russia has retained a tightly controlled society even as it transitioned from the totalitarianism of the Soviet Union. Freedom of expression, the right to assemble, and private property rights are all supposed to be protected. But in 2016, the Federal Assembly adopted laws to expand the power of law enforcement and security agencies. Association with an organization that is believed to undermine Russia's national security or constitutional order can result in fines or prison sentences. Public protests increasingly go unsanctioned by authorities, and people have been prosecuted for criminal extremism after social media or online posts. Protestors and dissenters are often labeled as "foreign agents" and charged with undermining national security.

Challenges to Russian elections have increased since 2000, with critics of the government and election process claiming that elections are not free or fair. The lead-up to and results of the 2018 presidential election, which saw Vladimir Putin win a fourth term in office, sparked demonstrations and protests against corruption. Police detained 1,600 protestors across the nation on the day of Putin's inauguration, many of them young people.

Freedom of Choice

Under the Soviet system, Russians did not typically have much choice over the direction their lives would take. A person's livelihood was determined by the collective needs of the country, not necessarily their personal interests or abilities. This has changed in that Russians have more control over their life decisions today.

Young men and women in Russia have traditionally been encouraged to marry as soon as possible. The minimum legal age

Russian citizens took to the streets before Vladimir Putin's inauguration in May 2018. The people protested the president as well as corruption.

Quality of Life   81

to marry is 18 years, but today there is a growing trend for young people to delay marriage until they have completed their education and begun their careers.

For several decades, state-financed abortions were the main form of birth control used by Russian women. By the beginning of the 2000s, the government began initiatives to slow the abortion rate by limiting access to abortion services, with support and lobbying by conservative lawmakers and leaders of the Russian Orthodox Church. This occurred, however, without improved access to contraception and family planning. The use of contraceptives has increased in Russia overall, indicating that women are taking advantage of opportunities to make choices about family planning.

Tolerance and Inclusion

Despite guarantees of protection in the Russian constitution, multiple groups have seen their rights impinged and their lives thrown into upheaval due to intolerance and discrimination. Practices of intolerance, discrimination, and, in some instances, persecution may not necessarily be state sanctioned, but policies and practice at the federal level have not protected the security of these groups.

Religious intolerance has historical roots in Russia. Today, the Russian government officially recognizes only a handful of religions. Religious minorities, particularly certain Muslim groups, Jehovah's Witnesses, and Scientologists, have experienced bans on their ability to worship or even complete the process to register with the state. Because religious affiliation is often entwined with ethnic identity, discrimination based on religion is sometimes a difficult motivation to identify and address.

Rates of immigration to Russia have increased through the first two decades of the 2000s. The influx of migrants is, in a way, welcomed by Russian authorities, as it provides a much-needed boost to the labor force. However, the majority of Russians are displeased with the arrival of migrants from outside Russia, particularly from poorer neighboring nations. Migrants are often seen as unskilled or poorly qualified, and the influx has raised fears of increased terrorism or extremism. Intolerance increasingly extends toward Ukrainians, no doubt stemming from geopolitical conflict in the wake of Russia's annexation of Crimea. There is

Discrimination against the LGBTQ Community

Long-standing discriminatory actions and policies against members of Russia's lesbian, gay, bisexual, transgender, and queer (LGBTQ) community have continued in the 2010s. This has included what has been termed "gay propaganda" laws, including the prohibition of positive information about LGBTQ relationships being shared with children. Violations of these laws have resulted in penalties such as large monetary fines, and LGBTQ websites can and have been blocked. The law has been used to stop LGBTQ pride marches and detain activists and is considered by critics as a move by President Putin to shut down dissent and improve relations with the Russian Orthodox Church. The European Court of Human Rights has ruled these laws to be illegal under the European Convention on Human Rights, which Russia ratified in 1998.

Homosexuality was a criminal offense until 1993 and considered a mental illness until 1999. The rate of hate crimes against LGBTQ individuals doubled between 2012 and 2017, with most of these crimes categorized as murders. Other actions against members of the LGBTQ community have included the detention of gay men; reports surfaced in 2017 that a "gay purge" was underway in Chechnya, wherein 100 men were detained and tortured based on their sexual orientation. Chechen authorities denied the allegations of persecution but also denied the very existence of gay men in Chechnya.

Although homosexuality is no longer considered a criminal offense, there appears to be targeted violence toward the LGBTQ community. In 2018, Russia's first gay pride parade event was cancelled within 24 hours of it being announced due to a law banning "homosexual propaganda" and demonstrations supporting gay rights. People across the world stood in solidarity with the Russian LGBTQ community at their pride parades.

Quality of Life

also concern that increased numbers of immigrants may spark already escalated ethnic tensions. Migrants face many struggles in their new country, including low wages, broken or nonexistent contracts, and inhumane working conditions.

Higher Education

Approximately 890 private and public institutions of higher learning were operating in Russia in 2016, with almost 4.8 million students enrolled in that year. The country has three categories of higher education institutions: institutes, which provide training for a single profession or undertake scientific activities; academies that offer training in a narrow range of professions, with a focus on a single industry such as mining or agriculture; and universities, which include technical colleges and classical universities offering a wide range of studies. Fifteen Russian institutes of higher education are globally ranked. The top 10 include the following:

- M. V. Lomonosov Moscow State University
- National Research Nuclear University MEPhI (Moscow Engineering Physics Institute)
- Novosibirsk State University
- Moscow Institute of Physics
- Saint Petersburg State University
- Saint Petersburg State Polytechnic University
- Tomsk State University
- National Research University—Higher School of Economics
- ITMO University
- Kazan Federal University

In 2012, more than half of Russian adults had earned a tertiary degree, the equivalent of a college degree in the United States and Canada. In 2016, over 89,000 women were enrolled in higher education institutions, with that number continuing to grow.

Nations in the News:  RUSSIA

Students attend a lecture at Moscow State University.

Text-Dependent Questions

1. What factors hinder people's access to quality health care in Russia?
2. Describe the overall purpose and goals of the Russian education system.
3. What role have immigrants taken in Russian society?

Research Project

Research which religious minorities face the greatest instances of discrimination in Russia. Choose one group, and complete a presentation highlighting the history of discrimination, governmental policies and practices (local, regional, federal) that affect the population, and actions and/or activities, if any, that have been undertaken by the minority group to ensure and protect the rights of the group.

Quality of Life

CHAPTER 5
Society and Culture

Echoes of past societal structures have long impacted the Russian populace. The split between the rich aristocracy and the poor peasants and serfs of the Russian Empire can still be seen in the gaps between the wealthy upper class and the working class. The fall of the Romanov dynasty in 1917 heralded in the Soviet era, under which Russians saw their place in society determined not by birth or ability but by governmental decree. The fall of the Soviet Union in 1991 brought with it a shift in the structure of society, government, and economics, and in the 21st century, Russia has continued its transition from the totalitarianism of the Soviet Union to a more democratic, civil nation.

In Russia, the family is the core of society and culture. Cultural values such as personal responsibility, service to the community, and cooperation between citizens have developed as Russia moves away from the collectivist mind-set of the Soviet era. Social organizations

Words to Understand

Homogenous: Consisting of parts that are all of the same kind or nature.

Pogroms: Violent attacks on Jews in the Russian Empire and other countries, carried out by local non-Jewish populations.

Russian Orthodox: A branch of Eastern Orthodox Christianity headed by the Patriarch of Moscow.

Nations in the News:

Much has changed in the Russia Federation since the fall of the Empire, but one thing remains the same—family is the core of society and culture.

Russia's Society and Culture at a Glance

Population	142.26 million
Sex Ratio	0.86 males/females
Age Distribution	17.12 percent age 0–14; 9.46 percent age 15–24; 44.71 percent age 25–54; 14.44 percent age 55–64; 14.28 percent age 65 and over
Ethnic Groups	Russian (77.7 percent); Tatar (3.7 percent); Ukrainian (1.4 percent); Bashkir (1.1 percent); Chuvash (1 percent); Chechen (1 percent); Other/Unspecified (14.1 percent)
Religions	Russian Orthodox, Muslim, other Christianity, Judaism, Buddhism
Languages	Russian, Tatar, Chechen

Whether they stay at home or take a walk in the park on the weekend, spending time with family is the most important thing to Russians.

like professional societies, veterans' groups, youth organizations, and women's associations continue to grow.

The sprawling geography of the Russian Federation encompasses multiple cross sections of society and culture, though most diversity is found in small numbers of ethnic, religious, and language groups. Overall, Russia's religion, language, and ethnic identity is **homogenous**, which has led to ethnic tensions as various minority groups struggle for representation, a place in leadership, or, in some cases, regional independence.

Birth and Death Rates

The birth rate in Russia stands at 11 births out of 1,000 people (2017), an increase from approximately 9.9 births for every 1,000 people in 2006. The infant mortality rate has decreased, going from 15.1 deaths per 1,000 live births in 2006 to 6.8 deaths per 1,000 live births in 2017.

Death rates have slightly declined, from 14.7 to 13.5 deaths per 1,000 people between 2006 and 2017. At present, the average life expectancy is 71 years. Men, on average, live to 65.3 years of age, while women live to 77.1 years of age.

A number of factors influence the birth and death rates, including but not limited to poor health conditions and inadequate access to preventative medicine in more remote areas of the country. Russia's death rate is much higher than the world average of nine deaths per 1,000 people, while the birth rate is half that of the world average (20 births per 1,000 people). Additionally, the fertility rate in Russia—1.3 births per woman—falls below the 2.1 births per woman needed to maintain a stable population, according to the World Health Organization. High abortion rates that have, in years past, outstripped the birth rate also contribute to Russia's overall population decrease.

President Putin addressed Russia's falling birth rate in 2006, when he called on the legislature to create a plan to increase the birth rate. Incentives included offering payments to couples willing to have more than one child.

Population by Age

Russia's population numbered 142.26 million people in 2017, making it the ninth most populous country in the world. When divided by age, the largest demographic segment is individuals ages 25 to 54, making up 44.71 percent of the total population. The next largest demographic is children up through 14 years of age, totaling 17.12 percent of the population.

Next are individuals ages 55 to 64 (14.44 percent) and 65 and over (14.28 percent); 9.46 percent of the Russian population fall between ages 15 to 24.

The average age for Russians is 39.6 years. Men have a slightly lower average age at 36.6 years, while the average age of women is 42.5 years.

Religions

Today's Russians identify with several religions, whether or not officially recognized by the government. Most people identify as Russian Orthodox—the official state religion—while Islam, other denominations of Christianity, Judaism, and Buddhism are recognized as traditional religions.

As of 2017, approximately 100 million Russians are Orthodox Christians. Islam is the fastest-growing religion at about 20 million worshippers and counting. Other major religions include Roman Catholicism, Judaism, and Jehovah's Witnesses.

Society and Culture

A Russian Orthodox priest leads his congregation in worship.

It is difficult to gather an estimate of other religions practiced in Russia, since a 1997 law requires religions to be registered with the government. Further, the Russian Orthodox Church's position as the official state religion grants it high levels of both social and political power; the decision to approve the registration of a minority religion can, in many cases, be decided by the Russian Orthodox Church. Unregistered religious groups face the possibility of bans on worship or even risk being labeled as extremist groups, seen as a threat to Russian unity and security.

Religion in Russia has a long history in which politics and faith intertwine at many points. Orthodox Christianity was adopted as the official religion in the 10th century, with the Russian Orthodox Church's patriarchs often influencing many of the Russian Empire's tsars. With the Russian Revolution came the general suppression of religious practices, though the Soviet Union's constitution guaranteed religious freedom on paper. Under Communism, churches had to forfeit property, and citizens were discouraged from being members of religious congregations. Religious activity increased with the fall of the Soviet Union, though many Russians are not active participants in the religions to which they adhere.

Ethnic Groups

The population of Russia comprises over 120 different ethnic groups. The nation's minority republics and autonomous districts and regions reflect the diversity of its people. Ethnic Russians make up the largest segment of the population—almost 80 percent—while other ethnic groups with more than one million members include the Tatars, Ukrainians, Chuvash, Bashkir, Chechens, and Armenians. Many of these ethnic minorities have lobbied for more autonomy from the government and even outright independence in some cases.

Since ethnic Russians still outnumber other minority ethnic groups, even in their own regions, ethnic conflict has been an issue for decades. A legacy of ethnic conflict can be traced back to the Russian Empire, when **pogroms** against the Jewish population of southern Russia and Ukraine occurred at several points in the 19th century. During Stalin's years in power, the push for all republics to remain loyal only to the USSR resulted in his appointing ethnic Russians to lead each republic. The policy continued through to the leadership of Mikhail Gorbachev; his appointment of an ethnic

A young boy reads the Qu'ran at the Moscow Cathedral Mosque.

Josef Stalin ruled the Soviet Union from the mid-1920s until his death in 1953.

Russian to lead the Communist Party in Kazakhstan sparked demonstrations and riots, which in turn incited the first example of ethnic violence in the Soviet Union where troops were deployed to suppress the dissenting populace.

Political transitions after the collapse of the USSR led to disputes over borders and decisions over who should lead, the rise of nationalism in the newly independent republics, and a surge in discrimination even as ethnic groups sought to reunify within restored national boundaries. Conflicts arose within and between territories, and in some cases resulted in Russian military intervention and a federal takeover, such as in Chechnya and Dagestan.

IN THE NEWS
Ukraine Accuses Russia of Changing Crimean Demographics

In February 2014, the Russian military intervened in Crimea, a peninsular territory that is strategically located on the Black Sea. The move, ordered by President Putin, was ostensibly in response to a political coup that ousted Ukrainian leader Viktor Yanukovych and his government. Yanukovych was considered pro-Russian, and concern surfaced about the many ethnic Russians living in the region.

The Crimean Peninsula had long been a disputed territory. With the arrival of Russian troops and the influence of Moscow, the Crimean legislature held a referendum to make Crimea an official Russian territory once again. The referendum passed, but it was seen as illegal by most of the international community. The Ukrainian government in Kiev decried the referendum and Russian takeover, and in 2016 the International Criminal Court released a report stating that Russia had violated treaties with the Ukraine and other aspects of international law by occupying Crimea.

Ukrainian officials claim that hundreds of thousands of ethnic Russians from Siberia have been relocated to Crimea, many of them military personnel and bureaucrats. Meanwhile, Crimean Tatars and Ukrainians are moving—or being pushed out. Russia denies the numbers put forth by Ukrainian analysts, saying its migration numbers are at a much lower level.

But Ukraine persists, citing extreme concern that the powers-that-be in Moscow are orchestrating a purposeful and forceful shift in the demographic composition of Crimea, something that would be considered a war crime under the 1949 Geneva Conventions if proven true.

Languages

Russian is the official language of the Russian Federation, spoken by 85.7 percent of the population. Other major languages spoken by citizens as reported on the 2010 census include Tatar (3.2 percent) and Chechen (1 percent). About 10 percent of the population speaks another native language, of which there are approximately 100.

Listen to a Russian language podcast.

Russian, Belarusian, and Ukrainian are East Slavic languages, part of the Indo-European language group. Old East Slavic was the language of the Kievan Rus, a loose federation of Slavic tribes in Eastern Europe that eventually became the first Russian nation-state. As the center of Russian power shifted to Moscow and the empire expanded, other indigenous languages in conquered territories were overwhelmed by the prevalence of the Russian language. It is expected that some of the languages spoken by indigenous and ethnic minorities will eventually disappear, since few are taught in schools.

Cyrillic: Russia's Written Language

The Cyrillic alphabet is based on the Greek alphabet and supposedly invented by Saint Cyril, a Greek monk who came to the area that is now Russia in approximately 860 CE and brought written language to Christian converts there for the first time.

Forty-four letters made up the original Cyrillic alphabet, with about 12 of them having been invented to represent Slavic sounds that do not appear in the Greek language. Peter the Great simplified and regularized the alphabet during his reign in the 18th century, removing several letters only used in Greek. Further changes were made in 1918. Today there are 32 letters in the Cyrillic alphabet.

Nations in the News:

Foods

Traditional Russian foods vary from region to region, due to the influence of different ethnic groups as well as climatic factors that influence the availability of ingredients. But across the nation, the staples of a Russian diet include potatoes, bread, eggs, meat, and butter. While fresh fruits and vegetables are difficult to come by, ingredients like cabbage, tomatoes, apples, cucumbers, and onions are common.

Bread appears on Russian tables in the form of rye bread, or black bread, and is a key part of the Russian diet. Traditional soups include *shchi*, made with cabbage, meat, mushrooms, flour, and spices, and borscht, made with beets and meat and served with sour cream. Buns called piroshki may be stuffed with either savory or sweet fillings, while blini are a traditional pancake served during festivals or religious rites, including wakes.

Rye bread, beef Stroganoff, borscht, and *shchi* soup.

Society and Culture

A woman stuffs dough with cabbage as she prepares piroshki.

Other common dishes include beef Stroganoff and a variety of fish-based dishes. Fish became a staple food due to the fasting days of Russian Orthodox Christians when meat could not be eaten. Fish is often eaten as an appetizer; it may be prepared by salting, pickling, or smoking.

National Holidays

Russia has nine official public holidays that are observed throughout the year. While some are connected to Russian Orthodoxy, others have political or historical meaning.

Religious Holidays

The religious holidays observed by Russians are Orthodox Christmas and Easter. Orthodox Christmas is held on January 7th; the difference in date between the Russian Orthodox Church and other Christian religions is due to the use of the Julian calendar rather than the Gregorian calendar. Christmas, overall, was not widely celebrated during the Soviet era, and even today is a relatively quiet holiday. Church services are a key part of the Christmas observance.

The Orthodox Easter observance varies from April to early May. Considered more important than Christmas in the Russian Orthodoxy, both the faithful and atheists attend Easter Mass. Russia's main Easter service is held in Moscow, at the Cathedral of Christ the Savior. As in Western cultures, decorative Easter eggs are a common symbol of the holiday and are traditionally painted red.

Civic Holidays

New Year's is the largest and most festive of Russia's civic holidays. While the holiday was once discouraged under the Communist regime of the USSR in an effort to remove religion from Soviet culture, eventually Soviet leaders resurrected New Year's as a secular event. It is marked by a two-week observance, spanning from December 31st to January 14th, that includes concerts, festivals, and an address from the Russian president.

Russia Day, or Independence Day, is celebrated each year on June 12th. This holiday marks the day Russia declared its sovereignty from the Soviet Union in 1991. Prior to 2002, the holiday

A priest blesses Easter eggs with holy water during the traditional paschal ritual.

Fireworks explode over Big Stone Bridge in Moscow on New Year's Eve.

was called "Day of Adoption of State Sovereignty of Russia" and was first observed in 1992. Complementing Russia Day, December 12th marks Constitution Day, which commemorates the adoption of the Russian constitution in 1993.

Victory Day falls on May 9th, and, like Victory in Europe Day (May 8th) in many Western European nations and the United States, it marks the yearly anniversary of the Allied victory over Nazi Germany in World War II. Celebrations are held in Red Square in Moscow each year, and Russians living in Ukraine also observe Victory Day.

Another public holiday, Unity Day, is held each year on November 4th. Unity Day calls for tolerance to be found between ethnic and religious groups across Russia. Its origins stem from an uprising in 1612 that freed Moscow from an occupation by Polish-Lithuanian forces.

Women's Day on March 8th is part of the larger worldwide observance of International Women's Day. Banks, government buildings, and schools are closed. The holiday was first observed in Russia in 1913, when Russian women staged a public demonstration demanding the right to vote.

Nations in the News:  RUSSIA

Soldiers march with the Russian flag in a parade to celebrate Victory Day.

Text-Dependent Questions

1. What factors have contributed to Russia's declining population?
2. How did government policies under Stalin and the collapse of the Soviet Union influence the development of ethnic conflict?
3. What challenges may be faced by religious groups that are not registered with the Russian government?

Research Project

Choose one ethnic minority found in Russia, and research the social and cultural history of its people. Be sure to include information about migrations, interaction with the Russian government, and historical circumstances that may impact that group today.

Society and Culture

Series Glossary of Key Terms

Absolute monarchy: A form of government led by a single individual, usually called a king or a queen, who has control over all aspects of government and whose authority cannot be challenged.

Amendment: A change to a nation's constitution or political process, sometimes major and sometimes minor.

Arable: Describing land that is capable of being used for agriculture.

Asylum: When a nation grants protection to a refugee or immigrant who has been persecuted in his or her own country.

Austerity: Governmental policies that include spending cuts, tax increases, or a combination of the two, with the aim of reducing budget deficits.

Authoritarianism: Governmental structure in which all citizens must follow the commands of the reigning authority, with few or no rights of their own.

Autocracy: Ruling regime in which the leader has absolute power.

Bicameral: A legislative body structured into two branches or chambers.

Bilateral: Something that involves two nations or parties.

Bloc: A group of countries or parties with similar aims and purposes.

Cash crop: Agriculture meant to be sold directly for profit rather than consumed.

Central bank: A government-authorized bank whose purpose is to provide money to retail, commercial, investment, and other banks.

Cleric: A general term for a religious leader such as a priest or imam.

Coalition force: A force made up of military elements from nations that have created a temporary alliance for a specific purpose.

Colonization: The process of occupying land and controlling a native population.

Commodities: Raw products of agriculture or mining, such as corn or precious metals, that can be bought and sold on the market.

Communism: An economic and political system where all property is held in common; a form of government in which a one-party state controls the means of production and distribution of resources.

Conscription: Compulsory enlistment into state service, usually the military.

Constituency: A body of voters in a specific area who elect a representative to a legislative body.

Constitution: A written document or unwritten set of traditions that outline the powers, responsibilities, and limitations of a government.

Coup: A quick change in government leadership without a legal basis, most often by violent means.

De-escalation: Reduction or elimination of armed hostilities in a war zone, often directed by a cease-fire or truce.

Defector: A citizen who flees his or her country, often out of fear of oppression or punishment, to start a life in another country.

Demilitarized zone: An area where military personnel, installations, and related activities are prohibited.

Depose: The act of removing a head of government through force, intimidation, and/or manipulation.

Détente: An easing of hostility or strained relations, particularly between countries.

Developing nation: A nation that does not have the social or physical infrastructure necessary to provide a modern standard of living to its middle- and working-class population.

Diaspora: The members of a community that spread out into the wider world, sometimes assimilating to new cultures and sometimes retaining most or all of their original culture.

Diktat: An order from an authority given without popular approval.

Disenfranchise: To take away someone's rights.

Displaced persons: Persons who are forced to leave their home country or a region of their country due to war, persecution, or natural disasters.

Economic boom: A period of rapid economic and financial growth, resulting in greater wealth and more purchasing power.

Economic reserves: Currency, usually in the form of gold, used to support the paper money distributed through an economy, available to be used by a government when its own currency does not have enough value.

Edict: A proclamation by a person in authority that functions the same as a law.

Embargo: An official ban on trade.

Federation: A country formed by separate states with a central government that manages national and international affairs, but control over local matters is retained by individual states.

Food insecurity: Being without reliable access to nutritious food at an affordable price and in sufficient quantity.

Free-floating currency: A currency whose value is determined by the free market, changing according to supply and demand for that currency.

Fundamentalist: A political and/or religious ideology based explicitly on traditional orthodox concepts, with rejection of modern values.

Gross Domestic Product (GDP): The total value of goods and services a country produces in a given time frame.

Hegemony: Dominance of one nation over others.

Heretical: When someone's beliefs contradict an orthodox religion.

Indigenous: Referring to a person or group native to a particular place.

Industrialization: The transition from an agricultural economy to a manufacturing economy.

Inflation: A general increase in prices and a decrease in the purchasing value of money.

Insurgency: An organized movement aimed at overthrowing or destroying a government.

Islamist: A military or political organization that believes in the fundamentals of Islam as the guiding principle, rather than secular law; often used synonymously (although not always accurately) with Islamic terrorism.

Jihad: A struggle or exertion on behalf of Islam, sometimes through armed conflict.

Judiciary: A network of courts within a society and their relationship to each other.

Mercantilism: A historical economic theory that focuses on the trade of raw materials from a colony to the mother country, and of manufactured goods from the mother country to the colony, for the profit of the mother country.

Migrant: A person who moves from place to place, either by choice or due to warfare or other economic, political, or environmental crises.

Militia: A group of volunteer soldiers who do not fight with a military full-time.

Municipal elections: Elections held for office on the local level, such as town, city, or county.

Nationalize: When an industry or sector of the economy is totally owned and operated by the government.

Parliamentary: Governmental structure in which executive power is awarded to a cabinet of legislative body members, rather than elected by the people directly.

Paramilitary: Semimilitarized force, trained in tactics and organized by rank, but not officially part of a nation's formal military.

Patriarchy: A system of society or government in which power is held by men.

Police state: Nation in which the state closely monitors activity and harshly punishes any citizen thought to be critical of society or the government.

Populism: An approach to politics, often with authoritarian elements, that emphasizes the role of ordinary people in a society's government over that of an elite class.

Propagandist: A person who disseminates government-created communications, like TV shows and posters, that seek to directly influence and control a national audience to serve the needs of the government, sometimes employing outright falsehoods.

Proportional representation: An electoral system in which political parties gain seats in proportion to the number of votes cast for those seats.

Protectionist: Actions on behalf of a government to stem international trade in favor of helping domestic businesses and producers.

Reactionary: A person who opposes new social and economic ideas or reforms; a person who seeks a return to past forms of governance.

Referendum: A decision on a particular issue put up to a popular vote.

Refugee: A person who leaves his or her home nation, by force or by choice, to flee from war or oppression.

Reparations: Payments made to someone to make amends for wrongdoing.

Republicanism: A political philosophy of representative government in which citizens elect leaders to govern.

Rubber-stamp legislature: Legislative body with formal authority but little, if any, decision-making power and subordinate to another branch of government or political party leadership.

Sanctions: Political and/or economic punishments levied against another nation as punishment for wrongdoing.

Secretariat: A permanent administrative office or department, usually in government, and the staff of that office or department.

Sect: A subgroup of a major religion, with individual beliefs or philosophies that divide it from other subgroups of the religion.

Sovereignty: The ability of a country to rule itself.

Statute: A law created and passed by a legislative body.

Subsidies: Amounts of money that a government gives to a particular industry to help manage prices or promote social or economic policies.

Tariff: A tax or fee placed on imported or exported products.

Theocratic: Of or relating to a theocracy, a form of government that lays claim to God as the source and justification of its authority.

Totalitarian: A form of government where power is in the hands of a single person or group.

Trade deficit: The degree to which a country must buy more imports than it sells exports; can reflect economic problems as well as strong buying power.

Trade surplus: The degree to which a country can sell more exports than it purchases; can reflect economic strength as well as poor buying power.

Welfare state: A system where the government publically funds programs to ensure the health and well-being of its citizens.

Chronology of Key Events

1480 CE	Mongols defeated and driven out of Russia.
1485	Ivan III consolidates territories, controlled from Moscow under autocratic rule.
1547	Ivan IV (the Terrible) becomes the first tsar; Russian expansion stretches east.
1549	Zemsky Sobor, the first Russian Parliament, created.
1565	The oprichnina, Ivan IV's seven-year reign of terror, begins.
1589	Russian Orthodox Church splits from other Eastern Orthodox churches.
1598	The "Time of Troubles," a 15-year period of social and political upheaval, begins.
1613	Mikhail Romanov elected tsar by the Zemsky Sobor.
1648	Russian explorers first cross the Bering Strait between Asia and North America.
1689	Peter I (the Great) becomes tsar and promotes Western culture.
1713	Saint Petersburg becomes the Russian capital.
1721	Peter I assumes the title of emperor.
1725	Death of Peter I.
1746	Nonnobles are banned from purchasing serfs.
1762	Peter III issues his "Manifesto on the Freedom of the Nobility."
1762	Catherine II (the Great) becomes Empress; Russia becomes a major European power.
1812	Napoleon Bonaparte invades Russia but is defeated and driven back to France.
1825	Decembrist uprising occurs.
1853	Crimean War; Russia is defeated three years later by British, French, and Ottomans.
1861	Start of reforms by Alexander II, including the abolishment of serfdom.
1867	The United States buys Alaska for $7.2 million.
1881	Alexander II assassinated; his son, Alexander III, begins a reactionary reign.
1894	Nicholas II becomes tsar.
1898	Russian Social Democratic Party established.
1904	Russo-Japanese War over control of Manchuria begins; it ends in a Russian defeat.
1905	Revolution breaks out; Russian people demand reforms in government.

1907	Russia joins the Triple Entente with France and Britain.
1914	World War I begins; Russia declares war on Austria-Hungary and Germany.
1917	Bolshevik Revolution; Nicholas II abdicates.
1918	Russia withdraws from World War I; Nicholas II and family murdered; civil war breaks out.
1922	Civil war ends with Bolsheviks and Lenin in charge; establishment of Soviet Union.
1924	Lenin dies; constitution of the USSR ratified.
1927	Josef Stalin comes to power.
1934	Beginning of Stalin's "Great Purge," resulting in the deaths of 20 million people.
1939	Nonaggression Pact signed with Germany; invasion of Poland; World War II begins.
1941	Germany invades Soviet Union; USSR joins the Allies.
1942	German army defeated at the Battle of Stalingrad, a major turning point in World War II.
1945	World War II ends; Soviet Union controls much of Eastern Europe, including East Germany.
1955	Warsaw Pact established between Soviet Union and seven of its satellite states.
1961	Building of the Berlin War; Russian cosmonaut Yuri Gagarin is the first man in space.
1962	Cuban Missile Crisis.
1979	Soviet-Afghanistan War begins; Soviets withdraw 10 years later in defeat.
1985	Mikhail Gorbachev begins reforms, democratization, and economic development.
1991	Soviet Union collapses; Russian Federation established under Boris Yeltsin.
2000	Vladimir Putin wins the presidential election; he will serve two consecutive terms.
2008	Putin steps down as president, named prime minister by successor Dmitry Medvedev.
2012	The election of Putin for a third term sparks protests and demonstrations.
2014	Russian forces invade Crimea; Crimea votes to secede from Ukraine and join Russia.
2018	Putin wins fourth term as president and states he will step down in 2024.

Nations in the News: RUSSIA

Further Reading & Internet Resources

Books
Allen, John. *Debates on the Soviet Union's Collapse (Debating History).* San Diego, CA: ReferencePoint Press, 2018.

Allen, John. *The Russian Federation: Then and Now.* San Diego, CA: ReferencePoint Press, 2014.

Beckman, Rosina (ed.). *The History of Russia from 1801 to the Present.* New York: Britannica —Educational Publishing, 2018.

Haugen, David. Russia (*Opposing Viewpoints*). Farmington Hills, MI: Greenhaven Press, 2013.

Kiesbye, Stefan. *Is There a New Cold War*? Farmington Hills, MI: Greenhaven Press, 2010.

Piper, Jessica. *Events That Changed the Course of History: The Story of the Russian Revolution 100 Years Later.* Ocala, FL: Atlantic Publishing Group, 2016.

Todd, Allen. *The Soviet Union and Post-Soviet Russia (1924–2000).* Cambridge, UK: Cambridge University Press, 2016.

Web Sites
Russia. *Country Profile. BBC News.* https://www.bbc.co.uk/news/world-europe-17839672

Russia. *Fast Facts. CNN.* https://www.cnn.com/2013/10/29/world/russia-fast-facts/index.html

Russia News. *Al Jazeera.* https://www.aljazeera.com/topics/country/russia.html

Russian Federation. *Country Profile. International Model United Nations Association.* http://www.imuna.org/resources/country-profiles/russian-federation

Russian History. *The History Channel.* https://www.history.com/tags/russian-history

The Face of Russia. *PBS.org* http://www.pbs.org/weta/faceofrussia/

Index

A
Afghanistan, Soviet defeat in war against, 18
agriculture, 62
al-Qaeda, 75
autocracy, 7, 8

B
banking system, 57–59
birth rate, 88–89
Bolshevik Revolution. *see also* Russian Revolution
  assassination of Nicholas II, 9, 37
  "Peace, Land, and Bread," 37
Brezhnev, Leonid, 10

C
Catherine the Great, 8
Caucasus Emirate, 31
Central Bank of Russia, 57–59
Chechnya
  conflict in, 18–19
  human rights abuses in, 12
  military occupation of, 30
  post-Soviet era, 11
  terrorist attack on Beslan school, 31
Chernobyl Nuclear Power Plant, 68
civil liberties
  freedom of choice, 81–82
  government controls on, 80–81
  limited by Putin, 11, 12
Clean Water project, 73
Cold War era
  beginning of, 10, 16
  defense industries, 63–65
Collective Security Treaty Organization, 24
collectivism
  in agriculture, 62
  defined, 54
commodities
  defined, 54
  export of, 66–67
conscription, 16, 30
constitution, 38–42, 44
Constitutional Court, 45
Council of the Federation
  establishment of in constitution, 39
  powers of, 49
crime rate, 75

Crimea, 12, 21, 24, 93
Cuban Missle Crisis, 10, 18
currency, 57
cyrillic alphabet, 94

D
death rate, 88–89
détente, 7, 10
drugs, illicit, 27–28

E
Eastern bloc, 16, 18
economy
  banking system, 57–59
  currency, 57
  exports, 54, 62–63, 66–67
  gross domestic product (GDP), 56
  imports, 66–67
  inflation levels, 62
  labor force, 59–61
  military budget, 28
  partial-market system, 54
  poverty rate, 61–62
  sanctions, 12, 56–57, 68
education
  institutions of higher learning, 84
  literacy rate, 77
  substandard medical training, 72
  system, 77–78
election process
  challenges to, 81
  changes by Putin, 11
  presidential elections, 47
energy production, 67–68
  renewable sources, 74
environmental issues, 79
ethnic groups, 91–93
Eurasian Economic Union, 24
European Union, 12

F
family planning, 82
Federal Anti-Corruption Law, 25
federation, 34
feudal system, 7, 8
fishing, 63
food, traditional, 95–96
forced labor, 26
forestry, 62–63
free trade, partial-market system, 60

 Nations in the News:

G

Georgia
  conflict in, 19
  military occupation of, 30
  post-Soviet era, 11
glasnost, 40
Global Peace Index, 75
Gorbachev, Mikhail
  appointment of ethnic Russian, 91–92
  economic reforms, 10–11
  glasnost, 40
  perestroika, 40, 42
  shift of resources to consumer industries, 63–65
gross domestic product (GDP)
  defined, 54
  in post-Soviet era, 56

H

health care. *see* medical care
HIV infection rates, 28
holidays, 96–98
homogenous, 86
human trafficking, 26–27

I

immigrants, 82, 84
industry, 63–66
Iron Curtain, 18
ISIS
  Russian intervention, 21–23
  terror attacks in Russia, 75
  terrorist attacks in Russia, 32
  war against, 13
Islamic State of Iraq and Syria. *see* ISIS
Ivan III, 8

J

jihad, 31
  defined, 16
judicial system, 45, 52–53

K

Khrushchev, Nikita, 63
Kievan Rus, 7–8

L

labor force, 59–61
languages, 93–94
legal system, 43–45
Lenin, Vladimir, 9, 16, 37
LGBTQ community, 83
life expectancy, 78–79, 88–89
literacy rate, 77

M

Marxist, 7, 9
medical care
  access to, 72
  birth rate, 88–89
  death rate, 88–89
  HIV infection rates, 28
  life expectancy, 78–79
  suicide rate, 79
Medvedev, Dmitry, 26, 47, 78
military, 28, 30
minimum wage, 60–61
Mongol, invasion of Russia, 8
Muscovite princes, 8

N

New START, 26
Nicholas II, 9, 16, 37, 51
Nixon, Richard, 10
nuclear weapons, 16, 26, 28
nutrition, 72

O

Obama, Barack, 26

P

Paris Climate Agreement
  defined, 70
  failure to meet parameters of, 79
partial-market system, 54, 60
perestroika
  defined, 34
  policy of Gorbachev, 40, 42
Peter the Great, 8
pogrom, 86, 91
political parties, 46
poverty, 61–62
prostitution, 26
Putin, Vladimir
  2018 reelection campaign, 13, 81
  democratic processes limited by, 11
  election process, 25
  fight against terrorism, 31
  minimum wage, 60–61
  Paris Climate Agreement, 79
  plan to increase the birth rate, 89
  presidential powers, 47–49
  term limits, 47, 48
  United Russia political party, 46

R

Regan, Ronald, 10
religion
  demographics, 89–90
  homogenous, 88
  intolerance, 82

Index 109

republicanism, 34
Romanov, 8, 86
Rurik Dynasty, 7–8
Russia Day, 42, 97–98
Russian Empire, 16
Russian Federation
  beginning of, 11
  constitution of, 38–42, 44
  corruption in, 25
  executive branch of, 47–49
  independence from Soviet Union, 42–43
  judicial system, 52–53
  legal system, 43–45
  legislative branch, 49–52
  official language of, 93
  political entities of, 24–25
  presidential powers, 47–49
  role of prime minister, 49
Russian Orthodox
  defined, 86
  official state religion, 89–90
Russian Revolution. *see also* Bolshevik Revolution
  dismissal of State Duma, 51–52
  establishment of totalitarian regime, 36
  Lenin, Vladimir, 37
  overthrow of Tsar Nicholas II, 16

S

sanctions
  damage to Russian economy, 68
  defined, 54
  by European Union, 12
  response to annexation of Crimea, 56–57
  by United States, 12
sanitation, 73
sex trafficking, 26
shelter, 74
Soviet Union
  Communist Party of the Soviet Union, 46
  economic development plans, 56
  establishment of, 9, 16, 37
  fall of, 11, 86
  foreign policy of, 26
  suppression of religious practice, 90
space exploration, 16
Stalin, Josef, 9, 37, 56, 91
State Duma
  defined, 34
  establishment of, 51
  establishment of in constitution, 39
  powers of, 49

subsistence
  defined, 54
  level of income, 61
suicide rate, 79
Supreme Court, 45
Syrian civil war, Russian involvement, 13, 21–23

T

terrorism, 31–32, 75, 76
tolerance, 82–84
totalitarian
  defined, 34
  regime resulting from Russian Revolution, 37
transparency
  access to information, 78
  defined, 70
tsarist
  defined, 7
  rule of the Romanovs, 8

U

Ukraine, conflict in, 21
unemployment rates, 59
Union of Soviet Socialist Republics (USSR). *see* Soviet Union
United Nations
  Russian membership in, 18
  Russian membership on Security Council, 12
  Security Council veto power by Russia, 26
United States
  economic sanctions against Russia, 12
  Russian meddling in presidential election, 7, 12, 23
unpotable
  defined, 70
  percentage of water sources, 73

W

water, drinking, 72–73
Women's Day, 98
World Health Organization, 72, 89
World Trade Organization, 18, 57

Y

Yanukovych, Viktor, 21
Yeltsin, Boris
  appointment of Putin as acting president, 48
  coup attempt, 42–43

Author's Biography

Jennifer L. Rowan teaches secondary social studies for Charlotte-Mecklenburg Schools in Charlotte, North Carolina. She holds two master's degrees, including a master of science in literacy education, and has over 12 years of teaching experience in New York and North Carolina. She is also a freelance writer and editor and an author of fiction. A native of upstate New York, near Syracuse, Rowan now lives in the greater Charlotte area with her family.

Credits

Cover

Top (left to right): Elena Masiutkina/Shutterstock; ID1974/Shutterstock; Martynova Anna/Shutterstock
Middle (left to right): Dmitry Nikolaev/Shutterstock; kojoku/Shutterstock; Mordolff/iStock
Bottom (left to right): Nikolay Gyngazov/Shutterstock; BONK! Photography/Shutterstock; Vladimir Wrangel/Shutterstock

Interior

1, Bo Li/Dreamstime; 6, Popova Valeriya/Shutterstock; 8, Jazziel/Shutterstock; 9, Meoita/Shutterstock; 10, Lagutkin Alexey/Shutterstock; 11, mark reinstein/Shutterstock; 13, Aygul Sarvarova/Shutterstock; 14, Popova Valeriya/Shutterstock; 17, Triff/Shutterstock; 19, Mikhail Evstafiev/Wikimedia Creative Commons; 20 (UP), Mikhail Evstafiev/Wikimedia Creative Commons; 20 (LO), Grisha Bruev/Shutterstock; 21, Anton Holoborodko/Wikimedia Creative Commons; 22, kafeinkolik/Shutterstock; 24, Creative Commons; 25, Sergei Primakov/Shutterstock; 27, Pete Souza [Public domain]; 29, Volkova Iuliia/Shutterstock; 30, M. A. Arkhipov/Shutterstock; 32, Wikimedia Creative Commons; 35, Tanya Kalian/Shutterstock; 36, Wikimedia Creative Commons; 38, sibfox/Shutterstock; 40, mark reinstein/Shutterstock; 41, mark reinstein/Shutterstock; 43, David C. Turnley/KRT/Newscom; 45, Free Wind 2014/Shutterstock; 46, Olga.Sh/Shutterstock; 48, Rostislav Ageev/Shutterstock; 50, ID1974/Shutterstock; 51, Everett Historical/Shutterstock; 52, VladKol/Shutterstock; 53, Martynova Anna/Shutterstock; 55, Vereshchagin Dmitry/Shutterstock; 56, blurAZ/Shutterstock; 58, Stanislav71/Shutterstock; 59, Tramp57/Shutterstock; 61, Ovchinnikova Irina/Shutterstock; 63, Pavel L Photo and Video/Shutterstock; 64 (UP), Nick Kashenko/Shutterstock; 64 (LO), Karasev Victor/Shutterstock; 65, Heinz Junge/Creative Commons; 67, ANGHI/Shutterstock; 69, knyazevfoto/Shutterstock; 71, Kekyalyaynen/Shutterstock; 73, Busurmanov/Shutterstock; 74, VPales/Shutterstock; 75, Pukhov K/Shutterstock; 76, Maya Zhinkina/newzulu/Newscom; 77, Papava/Shutterstock; 80, KDN759/Shutterstock; 81, De Visu/Shutterstock; 83, Alexandros Michailidis/Shutterstock; 85, Pavel L Photo and Video/Shutterstock; 87, Baleika Tamara/Shutterstock; 88, lornet/Shutterstock; 90, Denis Kuvaev/Shutterstock; 91, Nickolay Vinokurov/Shutterstock; 92, Wikimedia Creative Commons; 95 (UP LE), Gita Kulinitch Studio/Shutterstock; 95 (UP RT), Piotr Krzeslak/Shutterstock; 95 (LO LE), Andrey Starostin/Shutterstock; 95 (LO RT), vovidzha/Shutterstock; 96, Stanislav71/Shutterstock; 97, Alexey Borodin/Shutterstock; 98, aquarellinka/Shutterstock; 99, Alt Eduard/Shutterstock